The Hunted

Editor: Talia Leduc

ISBN-13: 9781990590849

Give feedback on the book at:
lorhainneeckhart@hotmail.com

Twitter: @LEckhart
Facebook: AuthorLorhainneEckhart

Printed in the U.S.A

THE HUNTED

THE O'CONNELLS
BOOK EIGHTEEN

LORHAINNE ECKHART

"I literally could not put this book down once I started reading... absolutely riveting, very thought provoking, and in the end, inspiring."

— REBMAY

"Deeply emotional & stirring."

— CATLOU

"A story telling the whole ugly and corrupt goings on within the justice system."

— C. Logue

About the O'Connells

The O'Connells of Livingston, Montana, are not your typical family. Follow them on their journey to the dark and dangerous side of love in a series of romantic thrillers you won't want to miss. Raised by a single mother after their father's mysterious disappearance eighteen years ago, the six grown siblings live in a small town with all kinds of hidden secrets, lies, and deception. Much like the contemporary family romance series focusing on the Friessens, this romantic suspense series follows the lives of the O'Connell family as each of the siblings searches for love.

The O'Connells

The Neighbor
The Third Call
The Secret Husband
The Quiet Day
The Commitment, An O'Connell Novella
The Missing Father
The Hometown Hero
Justice
The Family Secret
The Fallen O'Connell
The Return of the O'Connells
And The She Was Gone
The Stalker
The O'Connell Family Christmas
The Girl Next Door
Broken Promises
The Gatekeeper
The Hunted

When two prisoners escape and one is found dead, Marcus O'Connell finds himself being hunted—and the hunter could be someone he trusts.

One late night, Sheriff Marcus O'Connell receives a call about two escaped prisoners considered a danger to the community. A search is underway, and the warden has reason to believe the escaped convicts are headed toward Livingston. An urgent warning is issued: Shoot to kill.

Hours later, Marcus is called to a crime scene. The body of one of the escaped prisoners has been discovered deep in the woods, and the scene has already been lit up, with three prison guards standing over the body, along with the sheriff and deputy from the county over and a tracker with his dogs. A story has been neatly put together, and the group at the scene tries to send Marcus on his way.

Yet one prisoner is still missing. Marcus is told no investigation is necessary, that he should sign off on the case and walk away. But nothing adds up. The problem is that dead men can't talk, and Marcus can't shake the feeling that the story he's being told is a coverup for something far more sinister.

CHAPTER I

The sound of crickets punctuated the quiet neighborhood. Darkness had settled in, but Marcus needed a minute, as he leaned against the large porch beam, before he could lock up for the night and feel that all was okay in his part of the world. He lifted his hand in a wave to his brother Owen and his wife, Tessa, as they drove away in her small compact. Again, he took in the neighbors' houses. Next door, the lights were off and all seemed quiet.

Ryan and Jenny were already inside their house across the road, and the outside light was now off. Marcus waited for that feeling he got every night before locking up, an assurance that it would be okay for him to lay his head down and go to sleep. He counted heads, making sure everyone was okay, listening to the sounds inside his house, the fussing of Cameron, who was doing his nightly protest against going to sleep.

The screen door squeaked open behind him, and Marcus turned to see his dad step out, wearing blue jeans and a black t-shirt. He heard his mom and Reine talking inside. His dad nodded to him and headed over.

"Your mom is finishing up in the kitchen with Reine and Eva," Raymond said. "That boy of yours is just like you. You always fought your mom and argued every night about how you weren't tired, but a second later you'd be out cold. You didn't know how to stop."

Marcus turned to look back at the street. He was still trying to understand his dad. He leaned against the post on the porch, breathing in the warm summer night. The smell told him tomorrow would be another hot day.

"You were rather quiet tonight," Raymond said. "Everything okay?"

What was he supposed to say? This feeling had come out of nowhere. He couldn't remember ever having felt so unsettled, and he didn't have a clue what had caused it—family, life, something else?

"Just one of those days, you know," Marcus said, unable to find words to explain it.

His dad only nodded. It wasn't lost on Marcus that his dad had been forced to stick around Livingston because his mom had refused to leave her children and grandkids. His dad had a way of seeing everything. Marcus had figured that much out, but a stranger wouldn't have been able to tell, as Raymond never let his gaze linger too long.

Now he did, narrowing his eyes, peering out into the darkness. The stars were out, and a few streetlights were on. "Always the sheriff, looking out to make sure everyone is tucked in, safe," he said. "Expecting trouble?"

Marcus looked over to his dad. Inside, the house

phone was ringing, and a second later, it was answered. "You know something I don't?" he said. The sarcasm dripped.

His dad only shrugged. Marcus heard footsteps and pushed away from the post just as the screen door squeaked again, and Reine stepped out, her dark hair pulled back, wearing a peach sundress, barefoot.

"Marcus, it's for you," she said. "It's Therese." She held out the cordless phone.

Marcus didn't look over to his dad, who he knew was watching him in the way only Raymond O'Connell could. Marcus took the portable phone. "Thanks, Reine," he said, then waited as she walked back in the house. He put the phone to his ear, glancing only once to his dad, knowing his deputy called only if there was something he needed to handle. "What's up, Therese?"

"Sorry to call so late, Sheriff, but I have a message from the warden from Montana State. Two prisoners have escaped, and all he said was that they could be headed this way. I was about to call him back..." There was static on the line. His deputy was cutting in and out, as if she were driving.

"Hey, Therese, you're cutting out. You said two prisoners escaped from Montana State?" He was already walking back into the house and taking the stairs two at a time. Upstairs, Charlotte was reading to his son, whom he thought he heard jumping on his bed. Marcus was in his bedroom now, yanking open the closet door and opening the gun safe to retrieve his .357 SIG.

"Sorry, Sheriff," Therese said. "I'm about twenty minutes away, and the cell service is like shit out here.

Picked up the message on the way. All it said was that two prisoners escaped. The warden is..."

"Kellogg," Marcus cut in, fastening the holstered gun to the waistband of his jeans. As he closed up the gun safe, he pictured a man he'd met only a few times.

"I missed that part of the message," Therese said. "I'll give him a call and let you know what he says."

Marcus glanced to the open door. His wife now stood in the doorway. "No, Therese, I've got it," he said. "I'll have Charlotte check the message, and I'll give the warden a call."

She said nothing, and he noted her hesitation.

"Anything else?" he said, realizing it had come out rather short.

"No, that was all," Therese said. "You sure, Sheriff? I don't mind making the call. It may be nothing."

"Or it may be a lot," he said. "No, I've got this one." Then he hung up and held the phone out to Charlotte, taking in her wide eyes.

"What's going on, Marcus?"

He reached for his badge. "Prison break or something along those lines. Therese just called, said the warden at Montana State left a message. Two prisoners. I need you to get his number and play that message for me."

She was already nodding and dialing the office. Something about his wife handling phones and dispatching again settled him in ways he couldn't explain. She scribbled down the number on a pad of paper on the dresser just as his two-year-old son came running in, all smiles, appearing nowhere near ready to go to sleep.

Marcus reached for him and gave him a toss in the air, then held him and kissed his cheek. "Hey, you. Giving your mom a hard time? You're supposed to be asleep."

"Not tired."

"Yeah, well, you will be soon. Go get a book and get in bed."

"Here, Marcus, the number," Charlotte said. "The message is kind of garbled, but yes, it's something about two prisoners escaping."

He put Cameron down after kissing him again and reached for the paper and the phone, shaking his head over his rambunctious son.

Charlotte shook her head. "He's going to be the end of me. You know he argues every night about how he isn't tired?" She pulled her arms over her faded green t-shirt, her dark hair pulled up in a ponytail. "You're heading out, aren't you?"

"Yeah, after I call the warden," he said. "I don't like this."

There it was, that smile of hers he loved. She leaned in the doorway, glancing once over her shoulder down the hall to where their son's bedroom was as he dialed the phone.

"Montana State, warden's office." The voice was muffled, and Marcus had to really listen past the rough twang.

"This is Sheriff O'Connell, from Livingston. Is the warden there? I've got a message from him about a prison escape."

He heard a rustle on the other end, then a clunk. Evidently, whoever had answered barely knew how to use a phone. "Yeah, yeah," the person said, then yelled out, "Warden! Call for you from that Sheriff O'Connell."

Marcus reached for his wallet and stuffed it in his back pocket, then reached for his duty belt. Charlotte didn't look away, gesturing for an explanation, but Marcus only shook his head. There was another rustle on the phone.

"Sheriff? Warden Kellogg here." The man had a deep voice. "Afraid two prisoners escaped. Was discovered only a short time ago by one of the guards. We're in lockdown now. Just finished a count and are interrogating some prisoners. We know two got out for sure, but how, we have no idea. They likely had help from inside. I suspect they could be headed your way. These men are dangerous, both of them. I've already contacted state officials, as well, along with the other sheriffs in the area. An order has already been issued: Shoot to kill."

Marcus angled his head, looking right at Charlotte. He wasn't sure he'd heard the warden correctly. "You can't be serious," he said. "Who authorized that order? With all due respect, Warden, capturing the prisoners is the first priority."

"Sheriff O'Connell, these prisoners are a danger to the community," the warden said. "They will slit your throat and kill you without a second thought. If you want to dance around them and be the nice guy, do it on your own time and not at the detriment of the good people of Montana. You see them, you shoot them, because these two will do anything and everything to avoid capture. Killing, maiming, looting, burning. You want the details of what they'd do to your wife and sisters, everyone in your family, everyone you care about? If you want to argue with me about bringing them in alive, you can do it, but I don't want these two getting anywhere near innocent people. I've already reached out to Judge Harris, and photos of the prisoners have been sent to you."

Marcus didn't have a clue who these two prisoners were or what they'd done, but that sick feeling was back in his stomach with the image of the horror the warden had painted. Damn, what kind of evil had the two men done?

On the other end, the warden was talking to someone else. Then he addressed Marcus again. "Anything else, Sheriff? If not, I suggest you get your ass out there and start looking. Stan has faxed over the photos, and emails have gone out statewide."

Something about Warden Kellogg had always unsettled Marcus, but he couldn't put his finger on what it was. "Yeah, you said they could be headed my way. Why is that? They have family, friends, contacts here? I need all that information."

"Everything about both prisoners has been sent to you. One has a girlfriend, I understand, outside Livingston, and a brother up toward Billings. If that's all, Sheriff, I've got a fucking mess to handle here. You have any questions, get in touch with Sheriff Lester up in Stillwater County. He's got more on them, and he's been on this since word went out. And, Sheriff O'Connell? A word of advice. I understand you may want to give these men a second chance, but sometimes we're all better off if a criminal is six feet under. You understand?"

Yeah, he understood, but a knot twisted in his stomach as he looked over to his wife. He wondered if this explained the sick feeling he had or the cold sweat that had broken out up his spine. "Understood," he said. "I'll start looking." Then he hung up and tossed the phone on the bed.

"What is it, Marcus?"

Marcus counted the extra clips in his duty belt, then walked over to his wife and ran his hand over her shoulder. "Warden says the prisoners had help from the inside to get out. Says they're dangerous. Photos have been faxed and emailed. Can you access those? I'm going to ask Mom and Dad to stay until I get back," he said. It was just a feeling he had, the need to keep his family together. "See if you can pull up the prisoners' files, too. Warden said they've been sent. I want to know everything about them: who they are, what they did, and exactly how dangerous they are."

He hurried down the stairs, and Charlotte was right behind him. Raymond was back in the house, and he could hear his mom, Reine, and Eva in the kitchen. Marcus stepped off the bottom step, and Charlotte moved around him into the living room, over to the small desk where her laptop was.

"What's going on?" Raymond said as Marcus reached for his sheriff's jacket and lifted it from the hook.

"Marcus, I just sent the photos and files to your phone," Charlotte called out.

Marcus pulled his iPhone from his coat pocket and turned to his dad. "Can you and Mom stay?"

Raymond didn't seem surprised. He only nodded and said, "Yeah, of course. You worried about something?"

Marcus pulled out the keys to his cruiser. "Two prisoners have escaped and could be headed this way. Warden says they're dangerous, so much so that he wants us to shoot first and ask questions later, so I don't want to leave Charlotte, Reine, and the kids alone."

He knew his dad understood. "Yeah, you got it," he said. "You be careful."

Marcus thumbed through his phone and pulled up the photos his wife had sent. One was dark skinned, the other lighter, both with dark hair and brown eyes, the same bugged-out mugshot expressions. Their names were Rafe Jackson and Holter Donnelly. "Charlotte, send these to Harold and Ryan, too," he called out over his shoulder as he opened the door, and his dad was right behind him, holding the inside screen. "Charlotte has the photos," Marcus told him. "Take a good look."

Raymond nodded. "I'll call Ryan and Owen," he said.

Marcus lingered just outside. He didn't know what to say to his dad. Out of anyone, he knew Raymond had a handle on this. "Thanks," he finally said, then started down the steps. He heard the door close behind him and the lock flick closed.

He dialed his cell phone, walking straight for his cruiser and climbing in. As he tossed his duty belt and coat on the passenger seat, the phone rang once, twice…

"Okay, what did you forget?" Suzanne answered. He thought he heard Arnie fussing in the background.

"Put Harold on," he said, shoving his cell phone in the mount on the dash. He started the car.

"No can do," Suzanne said. "He's in the shower. What is it?"

There she went, playing interference. He knew she was still pissed at him because he wouldn't let her play cop in his county.

"You tell Harold to get the hell out of the shower and call me back," he said. "There was a prison break. This is serious shit, Suzanne. Charlotte just sent him the photos and files. I need him to dig into it and then meet me at the office. I'm not messing around. Have him call me. Can you do that?"

She was quiet for a second. "Don't take my head off, Marcus. Yeah, I'll tell him. Hey, big brother?" She always seemed to need to have the last word.

"What?" he said as he backed the cruiser out, ready to get off the phone. He flicked on the headlights and gave the vehicle gas, looking out into the darkness, knowing he'd be taking a second and third look at anyone he saw that night, scrutinizing who they were and what they were doing.

"Watch your back," she said.

He felt a smile tug at the corners of his lips. "Always do," he said. "Now have Harold call me."

Marcus ended the call before his sister could add one more thing. As he rounded the corner, feeling his own angst, he drove slower than usual and took a good, long look at the few pickups parked along the street, scanning for anyone out walking. There was only a couple with a dog.

This was going to be a really long night.

CHAPTER 2

Marcus stood outside the station in the dark, looking right and then left, tracking the headlights of a car as it went by. He heard the distant laughter of a few teens skateboarding just up the block. He was getting a sense for who was out, doing what, and where.

He pulled out his key and shoved it in the lock, then pulled open the door. The hallway was dark, but he didn't flick on the lights as he strode down it, his footsteps echoing. The lights were on inside the county sheriff's office, and he thought he heard voices.

When he opened the inner door, Therese was there, her dark hair pulled back, wearing blue jeans and a gray t-shirt. Colby, the junior deputy, was there too, which Marcus hadn't expected. He wasn't in uniform but instead wore a jean jacket over what he thought was a red t-shirt with a Confederate flag. Both were standing by Charlotte's desk and the fax machine, holding papers.

"Sheriff, the photos and files of the two prisoners

came in," Therese said. She held one for Rafe Jackson, the same one he'd already seen. "Colby just got off the phone with Sheriff Lester, who has all his men out looking."

Marcus dragged his gaze over to a quiet Colby. "And?" he said, taking in the young deputy's round face and eyes that were more brown than blue. Colby was lanky and tall, but Marcus still had a few inches on him. He hated this twenty-questions shit, and for a second, he didn't think Colby was going to divulge anything.

"He said not to worry about coming out," Colby said. "He has his men doing a grid search with the dogs, and he told me to pass along that you can stay close to home. They've got this."

Marcus just stared at Colby, then dragged his gaze to Therese. He couldn't shake the feeling that there had been a lot of discussion before he walked through the door.

The door opened behind him, and he expected Harold but glanced over his shoulder to see Suzanne, wearing the same blue jeans and bulky blue shirt under a faded old jean jacket, her long brown hair hiked high in a ponytail. She closed the door behind her.

"Where is Harold?" Marcus said. "Please tell me you're not bringing the baby, too."

Suzanne made a face only she could. "I'll have you know Arnie is at home, fast asleep, and so is my husband. I left him a note."

For a moment, he just stared at his sister, wanting to snap. She'd always been the hardest one to read. "Suzanne, this isn't the time for you to pull this crap. You understand there's been a prison escape? Call Harold.

You go home." He knew it had come out rather sharply, but he just turned back to Therese and Colby, who were watching the siblings with wariness. His frustration ramped up as he gestured at Colby. "And what were you about to tell me, Colby? You don't get to talk to another sheriff as if you're running things here. Sheriff Lester has no jurisdiction to tell you to pass along a message like that, as if I shouldn't worry my pretty little head."

"No, Sheriff, sorry, that wasn't what I meant," Colby said. "Or rather, it wasn't what Sheriff Lester meant. I'm sure he was just trying to be helpful, is all."

Now, why didn't Marcus believe that? "So that's it? That was all he said to you? You call him, or did he call here? Because I'm pretty sure my cell phone didn't ring."

Therese was now looking at Colby, and Marcus was starting to sense something else was going on.

Colby looked down to Charlotte's desk and the papers there. "I was here first, and there was a message from the sheriff. I called him, thinking I could get a head start on things before you got here, is all. He told me they're already on it and there's no need for you, that they have all the manpower they need. That's all, Sheriff. He was neck deep, and I could hear the dogs in the background. We didn't talk long."

Marcus glanced back to his sister, who had her arms crossed, watching Colby. She shot Marcus a significant look, and he heard himself let out a weary groan under his breath. He pulled out his cell phone. "I spoke with the warden," he said, "and he figures there's a girlfriend here in Livingston and a brother outside Billings. See what you can find out." He flicked his gaze to Therese, then over to Colby. "Both of you, start digging. What came through on these two?" He took in the message from his wife, a PDF, and tapped it open to see the mugshots of Jackson and Donnelly again, along with their arrest dates, prison records, and next of kin.

"We have a list of misdemeanors for both, nuisance charges, as well as trouble in prison," Therese said, holding out a paper with the same notes that had been on his phone. "Career criminals, by the looks of it. Verbal threats, assault involving a police officer, criminal mischief, unpaid fines..."

Marcus reached for the paper, because Therese had to be missing something, but it was truly just a bunch of petty misdemeanor charges. A pain in the ass, for sure, but not dangerous. The public defender had been the same for both of them, George Wallace, someone he'd never heard of.

"Therese, call the warden back and find out where the rest of the file is," Marcus said. "And call this public defender, Wallace, and find out from him what I'm missing about his clients. We were given an urgent warning, shoot to kill, which is not something I take lightly, and what I'm looking at here doesn't warrant that. I want to know what they haven't told me about how dangerous these two men are. I have a town full of people who have no clue about these prisoners on the loose. If anything, I need an alert put out to everyone in town to be on the lookout. You both got it?"

"Yes, Sheriff, absolutely," Therese said, already on her way to her desk. Colby was still holding some papers, which Marcus snatched from his hands, but they were just a duplicate of the misdemeanor charges, as if someone had just kept faxing the first page.

"Colby, you tell me everything that was said between you and Sheriff Lester?" Marcus said.

Colby looked up at him with wide eyes. "He was just rushed, impatient, is all. Sheriff, he said not to worry, that he's got it."

Marcus glanced back to his sister, who only shrugged and widened her eyes. She thought she was being coy, but he knew her better. He dragged his gaze back to Colby. "Yeah, well, I doubt that. He's got nothing in my part of the county. Go and give Therese a hand." He turned to his sister. "You, come with me."

Marcus headed for his office, hearing Therese on the phone already, wishing Harold were there. He waited as his sister walked into his office behind him, and he flicked on the light and closed the door behind her, holding the knob, taking a second. He walked over to his desk and dumped the papers on it.

"I know what you're going to say, Marcus."

"Oh, I highly doubt that," he said. Everything in his sister's face, her passion, her life, reminded him so much of the little girl who had tried to tag along on whatever he and Ryan had been up to as kids. They'd spent so much time ditching her, and it seemed she was still trying to find a way to sneak in, only now they were grown-ups, and she wasn't scared of anything.

"You don't have to be so nasty," she said. "Besides, you've got Therese and Colby out there, making calls for you. You really should get notice out to the public. You don't have to give details of what they've done, but you need their photos out there so people in the surrounding area know to be on the lookout and not open their doors for a stranger. We don't want someone to take the trash out and find one of these two hiding in their yard. People need to know to lock their doors tonight, Marcus, and maybe keep that shotgun in easy reach."

He just stared at his sister, knowing she was right, but it was only because she was messing with him and interfering in his business, police business, that he wasn't already all over it.

"Don't worry, Marcus," she said as she pulled open the door. "I can handle this for you, and then I promise you I'll call Harold."

He just stared at her. The phone was ringing from Charlotte's desk, and he heard Colby answer it. "Fine," he said. "Handle it. Get the notice out to local TV stations and cell phones, and then you call your husband and go home."

Whomever Colby was talking to, he was now writing something down. "Yes, I'll let the sheriff know," he said. "He'll be right out there." Then he hung up. Marcus had just stepped back around his desk when Colby lifted the notepad and called out to him, "Sheriff, they found them! One's dead, just past Miller's Field. They need you out there to sign off. I can tag along."

Marcus stared at Colby with a sinking feeling. Maybe it wouldn't be such a long night after all. "No, it's fine," he said. "You go on home. I've got this." Then he looked back to his sister, who was giving him that wide-eyed look. He shook his head and said, "You may as well come with me."

There it was, a smile. For a second, he wondered whether she'd do a victory dance.

"Don't get too excited," he said. "Just making sure you don't turn this office upside down."

"Now, don't be nasty, Marcus," Suzanne said, thumping his chest with her fist as she walked past him and pulled open the door.

Marcus glanced back over to Therese, who was now off the phone. "You too, Therese, head on home. I'll call you if there's anything else," he said.

Then he was out the door behind his sister, letting out a heavy sigh as he took in the paper he held. He knew well the location, a secluded spot in his county. His sister should have been home with her baby, yet there she was, sticking her nose in his crime scene.

"Well, are you coming, Marcus?" Suzanne called from the door and gestured impatiently.

"After this, you go home," he told her. "Better yet, I'll drop you off."

She only angled her head, then gave it a shake and fell in beside him as they walked out to his cruiser. Harold's Kia was parked right beside him.

"You didn't tell Harold, did you?" he said, though it wasn't a question.

Her hand was on the passenger door. Her mouth tightened, and she shrugged. "He really did fall asleep. I left him a note."

He shut his eyes as Suzanne opened the passenger door and climbed in. Yeah, he was going to have to have a word with his deputy about dealing with his sister. He slid behind the wheel and started the car. "When we get out there, Suzanne, I want you to stay out of the way."

"Whatever you say, Marcus," was all she said, and he knew she didn't mean it. Damn, at times, he really did have a ton of sympathy for Harold.

CHAPTER 3

"Is that it?" Suzanne said. "Holy shit, Marcus, it looks like everyone's here. What did Colby say happened, again?"

Marcus parked behind a sheriff's cruiser from Stillwater County and took in how many vehicles were on the scene just off the dirt road, surrounded in bushes and trees—another sheriff's cruiser, a few pickups, and a van with *Montana Corrections* on the side. What had to be the crime scene was flooded with light. He shoved the vehicle in park, feeling his anger spike, because he wondered how many of them had missed the fact that they were now treading in his territory. Suzanne was staring out the window, glued to the scene. Yeah, he really wished she weren't there.

"All he said was that it's a crime scene," he said. "I didn't expect this. Like, what the hell? This is clearly on my side of the county line." He stepped out of his cruiser and could just make out a sheriff's deputy walking his way. It was a face he'd never forget. "Lonnie," he bit out, still pissed that Sheriff Lester over in Stillwater County had hired the deputy without so much as a damn courtesy call. Lonnie had been a source of misery for Marcus, considering how far the man had gone in trying to destroy his family.

"Marcus, we've got this all handled here," Lonnie called out, actually raising his hands and waving as if Marcus were some bystander, as if he had any hope in hell of stopping him. Lonnie seemed to puff out his chest as he came to stand in front of him, sporting a mustache now. He settled his hand on his duty belt, another reminder of his arrogance. Then he held an arm out to stop Marcus from walking past him. "Whoa, stop right there."

"You seem to forget yourself, Lonnie," Marcus said. "This is my county you're in. You ain't handling nothing in my county. Now move the hell out of my way. You're out of your jurisdiction with no authority. You hear me?" Marcus leaned in, biting the last part out.

He took a step and realized Suzanne was right there beside him. Of course, she hadn't stayed in the car. Lonnie dragged his gaze over to her, lingering a little too long.

"Hey, Lonnie," she said. "It's been a long time."

Marcus didn't look away. He couldn't believe how calm Suzanne sounded.

"You keeping well, Suzanne?" Lonnie said.

Marcus gave his head a shake. "Fuck," he bit out, then stepped around Lonnie, bumping him, and glanced back at his sister. "Let's go," he said, knowing he sounded pissed off.

He kept walking, and Suzanne fell in beside him. He couldn't help glancing back to Lonnie, who was actually looking into his cruiser. "Fucking asshole! I swear, he puts one print on my cruiser and I'll take him down."

"Seriously, Marcus, let it go," Suzanne said. "He was just flexing his non-existent muscles, making up for the fact that he was castrated as a kid and has nothing for balls—not real ones, anyway. You think I haven't had to put up with those asshole moves? Just let it go."

He couldn't believe his sister sometimes. She kept up with him, her long legs matching his stride, hearing the crunch of debris, sticks, and leaves under his feet. It was still warm out. The trail was wide, and he passed another pickup, a four by four with the Stillwater County sheriff's logo. At another vehicle, a man had the back gate down and was loading three dogs in, two of them barking.

"Romi, who called you out?" Marcus said.

The dog handler was a big man whose dark hair had a natural messy wave. His beard was braided, his glasses were thick, and his belly was hanging over his belt. "Sheriff Lester over in Stillwater County called me," Romi said. "Got a call from the prison, too. Been a while since I had the dogs out, chasing someone down. Sheriff's over there. He asked me to hold tight and pick up the trail again for the other guy. The dogs need a break and some water, anyway. I told them if they keep tromping all over the scene, it makes it hard for the dogs to pick up the scent. It's been a long night so far, and it's about to get longer, I suppose."

Marcus took in the dogs in the back of the pickup. Two were now drinking water from an old tin bucket, and one was lying down. Under the floodlights just ahead, he spotted Lester with a bunch of other cops he didn't recognize. "Hold that thought," Marcus said, "and don't do anything until I give the word. This is my county, and any order to do anything comes from me first. Let me get up to speed here. One is caught, you said?"

"One is dead." Romi gestured with his thumb, and even though it was dark, Marcus didn't miss the disgust all over his face, though for what, exactly, he didn't know.

"Don't go far," Marcus tossed out over his shoulder as he started walking to the lit-up scene. His sister had again fallen in beside him.

"How friendly are you and this sheriff?" she said.

"He's tolerable, barely, considering he went behind my back in hiring Lonnie. Haven't had to deal with him too much. He stays in his county, and I stay in mine. Now this..." He gestured to the scene and the six people he counted ahead.

"Marcus," Suzanne said quietly, gesturing to Sheriff Lester, who was now walking his way, sweat stains on his brown uniform shirt and a sheriff's badge pinned to his chest. He was balding, heavyset, and gestured to someone behind him who had called out.

Sheriff Lester took off his hat and wiped the sweat from his forehead. The other man, the one who had called out, was in a ball cap and blue jeans, no one he'd ever seen before, another person in his county who should have been talking to him first. He was now walking the other way, though where to, Marcus had no idea.

"Well, Sheriff, sorry to drag you all the way out here and waste your time," Lester said. "We caught one of the bastards—or found him, really. Not much for you to do here. We kind of got this all handled. Body bag will be here in a minute. We'll toss the poor bugger in it, and the prison can deal with the remains."

Marcus stopped and looked past the sheriff, who was a few inches shorter than him. In a circle of trees, a man lay face down, arms at his sides. One of Lester's deputies was kneeling down over the body, and floodlights lit up everything. "I heard he's dead," Marcus said. "Just one, so the other is still on the loose?"

"Yup, afraid so," Lester said. "That one's Donnelly. Poor miserable soul, evidently not the smarter of the two." He actually tsked under his breath, then looked at Suzanne but said nothing, and his silence only put Marcus further on edge.

Three other men stood by the body in uniforms, so he stepped around the older sheriff, but his hand slapped right to his arm, stopping him. Marcus let his gaze fall there, and the sheriff pulled it away.

"Again, Marcus, we've got this handled. You just need to sign off and we'll finish up here. The guards will get the body hauled out, and everyone can go on home."

"You don't mind if I have a look, do you?" Marcus said. "After all, this crime scene is in my county. As you said, you need me to sign off. Seems you're working pretty hard to send me on my way, which has me wondering why. And a word of advice? Don't put your hands on me again."

His pissed-off voice had held a clear warning, and the sheriff lifted his hands and made a face, taking a step back. Marcus glanced over to his sister again, who, he realized by her widened eyes, had evidently picked up on the fact that something was wrong. She joined him in stepping around Lester.

"Now, don't go getting all hot and bothered there, Marcus," Lester said, turning to follow them. "We've already done all the heavy lifting here. Would think you'd be happy to just hop on home, crawl back in bed with that pretty little wife of yours, and have a good night's sleep."

Suzanne slapped her hand right to Marcus's chest before he could say anything. The old sheriff had fallen in beside her. Evidently, she knew Lester was really stepping into it with Marcus.

Marcus realized three of the uniformed men ahead were prison guards, likely from the state prison, men who worked for Kellogg, one taller than the other two. They only nodded once to him, but no one said anything, and everyone had a look that put him on edge just a little more.

Marcus took in the four spotlights lighting up the scene. The man was facedown, unmoving. There was blood on his back, and instead of an orange jumpsuit, he wore dirty brown prison garb, pants and a short-sleeved shirt. His dark hair was messy, short. Marcus didn't have a clue what had happened.

"So is someone going to fill me in?" he said. "I take it

this is one of the escaped convicts. Bullet in the back, lying facedown, dead. Who did this? A man shot in the back poses a problem."

The prison guards said nothing but exchanged the kind of look that had the hair on the back of Marcus's neck standing up. A deputy who had been leaning over the body walked over to him. He was of medium height and build, wearing a Stillwater County uniform, and had short dark hair.

"Jim Carlyle, Sheriff," he said, pulling off his rubber gloves to hold his hand out to Marcus in the first show of respect he'd received since arriving at the scene. Marcus hesitated only a second before shaking his hand.

"So what happened here?" Marcus gestured to the body, waiting for someone to start talking. He glanced behind him to the three men from the prison, standing together. What was it about having his back to them that really unsettled him?

"He was hiding," Sheriff Lester said, stepping in. "Came out of the bushes and took a swing at Peters over there. Lonnie shot him before he could do anything else. Dead by the time he hit the ground. Good thing Lonnie was there, or Peters could've been the one lying dead. Dangerous motherfuckers. Look, we chased him for miles on foot. He was a danger to the community, and the community is better off and far safer. He'd have raped, murdered, and done worse to any woman and child out there. This is better for everyone."

Marcus could just make out Lonnie standing over by his cruiser. He spotted emergency lights pulling up, likely for the body. He turned back and looked at the ground, the debris, leaves, twigs. His sister was staring at the body, and her blue eyes flickered with something he was familiar with. She had the same questions he did, maybe. At least she was staying quiet, or maybe she realized he wasn't in the mood to handle her, as well. It seemed Lester was speaking for everyone there.

Marcus stepped around Deputy Carlyle and angled his head as he took in the body again.

"Marcus, I understand your apprehension," Lester said, "and I'm very aware this is your county, but we're on the same team here."

"Oh, I doubt that very much," Marcus snapped, glancing back over to him. Lester had been sheriff in Stillwater County for as long as Marcus could remember. He wondered which residents kept electing him.

"Now, don't go getting all territorial," Lester said. "You're still new at being a sheriff, so you haven't learned how things work here. You back us up, Marcus. Don't go making this into something it's not, because the folks around here won't appreciate their sheriff wasting tax dollars and putting resources into a criminal who has already taken so much from so many. He's dead, caught, and that's all they care about. They don't want this dragged out or stirred up, creating a problem. The investigation is done, you hear me?"

He heard the warning in the old sheriff's voice, but he didn't miss the awkwardness in Jim Carlyle's stance, and then there were the guards, who had said nothing at all. He let his gaze linger on Lester. The man was doing his best to tell Marcus how to run his county and shut down questions about what had really happened there.

"Which one of you is Peters?" Marcus said, then waited. The one in the middle nodded. He was round in the middle, a few inches shorter than Marcus, and he realized none of them carried a weapon.

"That's me," the man said, then actually stepped forward and lifted his hand in the air. His hair was a lighter shade of brown, with messy waves. The other two guards had dark skin, one lighter than the other, one a few inches taller than the other, but both offered nothing, watching silently.

Lester appeared in his line of sight again, over by the guard, close to losing it on him. Evidently, he had missed the fact that Marcus was the kind of cop who actually did his own homework and allowed no one to tell him how to do his job.

"Well, how about you tell me what happened here?" Marcus said. He rested his hand over his duty belt, not missing the way the deputy glanced over at the sheriff.

"Just like the sheriff said, Donnelly sucker-punched me, knocked me down, and Lonnie took him out before he could take one of us out."

Marcus let his gaze linger on Peters. He heard approaching voices. One he knew was Lonnie, with the arrogant twang that had always irritated the shit out of him. He glanced over his shoulder to see a man in a jacket, the coroner, walking toward him as well.

Marcus dragged his gaze back to Peters and Sheriff Lester, who was watching the guard closely. Marcus figured the men would do what their sheriff said and go along with everything he told them to do. Again, that off feeling just wouldn't go away. He looked down at the body. The blood that covered the man's back and the ground appeared dry.

"So you're telling me he hit you?"

The guard hesitated, then nodded.

"Knocked you on your ass? And you were running around out here without a gun?"

The guard hesitated, narrowing his gaze. "Look, of course I had a shotgun. It's secured now, back in the vehicle. Sheriff, this was a long chase, and he wasn't about to go quietly. These are dangerous men. It could go down only one way."

Marcus pulled out his phone and opened the camera to take photos of the body, then walked around to the head. The man's arms were by his sides. Marcus crouched down and then gestured to Deputy Carlyle. "Roll him over," he said. "You have another pair of gloves?"

Carlyle pulled gloves from his back pocket and held them out to Marcus, who snapped them on. The sheriff was saying something to the guards, all three of them talking in low voices. The deputy leaned down and helped him roll the body over. He was very aware the crime scene was both compromised and clean. The prisoner's face had bruising, nothing fresh, and blood covered the front of the shirt. He found himself looking for an exit wound, aware that everyone was watching him.

"It looks like someone worked him over pretty good," he said.

"Prison life is hard," one of the other guards drawled.

Marcus didn't bother looking up. "Maybe so," he

said. "You say he came out swinging, hit you? From here, it doesn't look like you have a mark on you. You look like you have at least thirty pounds on him, give or take, but not a mark or a speck of dirt other than stinking of sweat? You don't look like a man on the receiving end of a fight. If it went down as you said, the prisoner should have been lying in a pool of his own blood, but the ground is dry, and the way he was lying on the ground, his hands at his sides, it seems as if he didn't even try to break his fall, almost as if he were placed there..."

"Now, you just wait a minute, Sheriff O'Connell," Lester snapped, fire in his eyes as he stepped over to Marcus, right in the circle of a crime scene that no one seemed too concerned about keeping clean. Marcus already knew without a doubt that everything had been tampered with, but could he prove it? No. "You accusing us of lying? If I were you, I'd think real long and hard about what you say next. You forget about what a danger this man was? A shoot to kill order was issued, so we took that motherfucker out, and no one is going to question us—not the warden, who ordered it, or Judge Harris, who signed off on it. You and I both know there could be a lot of reasons for the way we found him, including the fact that he was dead before he hit the ground. The blood could have soaked into the soil. And he sucker-punched Peters in a low blow to the groin. You want him to drop his pants so you can inspect him?"

Lonnie still stood with the coroner, and everyone was watching Marcus as if he were the problem. He realized he was the odd man out. He dragged his gaze over to Suzanne and her horrified blue eyes, and he just couldn't shake the feeling that time was up. She was in way over her head, and he needed her out of there.

"Marcus, the only one who has a problem here is you," Lonnie said. "This was a dangerous criminal that the world is a safer place without."

Marcus knew he made a face as he pulled off his gloves, standing up. "You shot a man in the back, Lonnie."

"Shoot to kill was the order, Marcus, or would you rather it were one of us lying there, dead?"

Lester pulled his hand over his chin and took a step closer to him, dragging his gaze from Lonnie to him. "Lonnie is right, Marcus," he said. "It was him or one of us, and I can tell you there was no goddamn way one of us was going down. You don't take chances with criminals who pose a danger to the good people of your county. I'm going to save you before word gets out in Livingston that the sheriff is more interested in protecting dangerous criminals than the people who elected him.

"This is how it's going to work, son: You're going to sign off on this, and we're going to handle all the paperwork, and then this thing is going to get filed away neatly. There's nothing for you to see here, nothing other than an escaped convict. This is about your ego, is all. I know there's bad blood between you and Lonnie, but set it aside, Marcus. Shake hands about this and move on."

Marcus couldn't believe the old sheriff was seriously treating this like some schoolyard disagreement. He let out a rough laugh and shook his head. "Un-fucking believable," he said under his breath, then dragged his gaze back to the sheriff and over to the three guards. Lonnie still stood with the coroner, who was holding a folded-up body bag. "Two prisoners, one dead, the other still on the loose."

His cell phone started ringing, and he saw Harold's name on the screen. He handed his sister the phone and said only, "It's your husband." She took it and stepped away to answer, and Marcus turned back to the sheriff and said, "So that's it?" He gestured to the body and to Deputy Carlyle, who was standing off to the side.

"As soon as you let it be and stop holding everyone up here," Lester said. "Oh, and, Sheriff? No need for you to join in the hunt for the other prisoner. Romi has his dogs ready, and we'll track him in no time. He couldn't have gone far. We'll find him."

Calm, cool. The way the sheriff let his gaze linger on Marcus, he knew he was done there. He tossed his gloves to Carlyle, who caught them one-handed, and then he took one step and then another over to the sheriff standing in front of him.

Marcus jabbed his finger at Lester's chest. "You come into my county again and pull this bullshit, you and I are going to have more than a problem, and you do not want that," he said. Then he glared at Lonnie, who stared at him with an arrogance Marcus wanted to wipe off his face.

He glanced over to Suzanne as she hung up, her back to him. The tension lingered, but he figured Harold had spoken his piece and then some. Marcus headed over to her and took his phone back.

"Let's go," was all he said as he started walking, and

Suzanne fell in beside him again, glancing back only once. "Everything okay?"

"Sure, other than the fact that Harold is likely ready to file for divorce," she said. "He demanded I get my ass home. Oh, and he asked me if I've lost my mind, considering Colby just called and filled him in, and that was when he saw my note."

Marcus glanced down at his sister. "Harold isn't going to divorce you. Don't be so damn dramatic."

She shrugged and nudged him. "No, he'll get over it. You're right, he loves me. But thanks for letting me tag along," she said, her voice light.

He glanced down at his little sister, who, at times, knew how to push every one of his buttons, and grunted, "Don't let this go to your head, but thanks for the extra set of eyes out there."

And for just being there to watch his back, he thought, but he wasn't about to tell her that last part.

Suzanne wrapped her arms around him, hugging him, and Marcus stumbled a bit. "Yay! Does that mean I can join the department?" She pulled back and tapped his arm with her fisted hand. He always knew when she was excited. Deep down, she was still a tomboy.

"Hell, no. I just have a feeling that if I'd shown up alone, this could have ended differently."

Suzanne glanced back, unsmiling. They kept walking past Romi, who was leaning over the back of his pickup, running his hand over one of the dogs, talking on his cell phone. He only lifted his hand in a wave to Marcus as he walked past.

"Yeah, about that," Suzanne said. "So who do you think moved the body, staged the scene?"

He shook his head, glancing again to his sister as they reached his cruiser. She walked around to the passenger side, and as Marcus climbed in and closed his door, she reached for her seatbelt. He pulled his keys from his pocket, shoved them in the ignition, and started it, considering everything that had happened, the scene, the night, and everyone who had been there.

He let out a sigh as he dragged his gaze to his sister. "Good question," he said. "My guess? All of them."

CHAPTER 4

As Marcus drove outside Livingston on a highway that went for miles, bordered by forests, mountains, privacy, and lots of places to hide, his mounted cell phone was ringing again, Harold's name on the screen. It was dark in the car, but he knew Suzanne saw it. He pressed the green answer icon.

"You know where we are right now?" was all Marcus said when he answered, hearing the baby crying in the background.

"Yeah, well, not much I can do, where I am. You're bringing Suzanne back? Can't even pack Arnie up because she took my car."

Marcus winced at the way Harold had snapped. Yeah, he was pissed, and could he blame him? Marcus kept on the road, his brights on the empty highway. His sister was quiet as he looked over at her, shaking his head again.

"Call my mom," Marcus said. They were getting

closer to Livingston. "She can send Jake over to pick up Arnie. Your car's at the station. Just left the crime scene, where Donnelly's body is. Goddamn Lonnie was there, put a bullet in his back. The way the body was laid out neatly, someone put it there. He was shot somewhere else. Makes no sense, considering the order was shoot to kill. Still don't know why, and you know me; I don't like puzzles where there are no answers. No one seemed too willing to come clean on what really happened. I smell a ton of bullshit, and the hunt is still on for the other prisoner, Rafe Jackson. If it's all the same, I'd like to find him first."

"Forget your mom," Harold said. "I already called Owen. He and Tessa are on their way over and will watch Arnie. Suzanne, you listening? You can't keep pulling this shit. A fucking note. You left a note about an active manhunt."

Marcus turned to his sister again. They had reached a point where this wasn't just between her and Harold anymore. "You two can hash that out later," he said. "You spoke to Colby? He filled you in on what the prison sent over on those two? Because I remember the warden saying something about a girlfriend in the area and a brother up by Billings, but I didn't get the details on them. Can you get me her address? And which one's girlfriend is she? Also, I told Therese to call the warden back and get me the rest of the file, because what they sent was nothing. They based a shoot to kill on a bunch of threats and misdemeanors. I'm missing something, and I don't like these kinds of holes."

"Look, I talked to Colby," Harold said. "He said

Therese put in a call to the warden but didn't talk to him. Had to leave a message. He didn't tell me you were missing information. I guess if someone had actually woken me, I could have been at the station, handling this already, and we wouldn't be two steps behind." Harold paused. "Owen and Tessa are here."

Marcus heard voices. Evidently, Harold was answering the door. The baby was still fussing. Suzanne said nothing, and when he glanced her way again, she stared straight ahead. Yeah, she was tough to crack.

"Well," Marcus said when Harold had come back on the line, "get your ass to the station and dig up everything on those two, but get me the girlfriend's address first and information on any other next of kin for Rafe Jackson. Everything on Donnelly, too."

Headlights were coming his way. Marcus flicked his brights as the car passed. His phone beeped, another call on the line.

"Harold, someone is calling," he said. "Just let me know when you're at the station." He hung up before his deputy could say anything else and answered the other call. "Marcus O'Connell."

"Sheriff, I just got off the phone with the public defender, George Wallace." It was Therese. "He couldn't recall the names. Said he'd have to pull the files and he'd call me in the morning."

"You tell him to get his goddamn ass out of bed and dig out those files now, not in the morning," Marcus said. "Does he have no fucking idea what the hell has happened? Two of his clients broke out of prison, there is a shoot to kill order, and one is dead." Damn, he was so done with no one giving him the answers he needed.

"Which, if you would have let me finish, was exactly what I told him," Therese said. "And I told him to call me right back." She sounded rather calm in response, considering he'd just taken her head off.

"Colby still there?" he said.

"Uh-huh. Told him to start digging around in the Corrections database."

Okay, so she'd been thinking.

"Oh," she said. "It's the public defender calling back."

He heard a phone ringing. "You know what, Therese? Put him through to me, and keep digging. And, by the way, Harold's on his way in." He glanced over to Suzanne in the darkened cruiser and realized she was looking right at him, shaking her head.

"Sure, I'll put him through," Therese said. Then she hung up, and Marcus glanced again at his sister.

"You know, Suzanne, stepping between you and Harold is not what I'm interested in doing, but you can't pull this. He's right. I depend on him. He's one of the best investigators out there, and he finds things I wouldn't think to have him look for. He's that good."

His cell phone started ringing again, and Suzanne said nothing. She was getting hammered from all sides. He pressed the green answer icon.

"This is Sheriff O'Connell."

"Sheriff, this is George Wallace, public defender. One of your deputies called about two prisoners I represented, a Rafe..." He was flipping through papers. His voice was a little too soft, too abrupt.

"Rafe Jackson and Holter Donnelly," Marcus said. "Donnelly is dead, by the way. Just left the scene. Jackson is still on the loose, so I need you to tell me why there's a shoot to kill order on them both, considering the only thing I received from the warden was a history of verbal threats, assault involving a police officer..." He could see the edge of Livingston and its lights.

More papers were flipping. "Oh, here it is," Wallace said. "Well, this doesn't make sense. You said who was dead?"

Damn, a confused public defender.

"Holter Donnelly," Suzanne said, jumping in. "Gunshot to the back. Was he a danger to the community?" Then, maybe because the public defender didn't know who was talking, she added, "This is Suzanne O'Connell."

Marcus wanted her to just stop, already.

"Okay, yeah," Wallace said. "I remember these two now, but I hope you know I can't share anything with you. Client confidentiality..."

"I'm not asking you to breach confidentiality," Marcus said. "What I'm asking for are the charges. Explain to me what this is. Were they a danger?"

He heard a heavy sigh in the background, then papers shuffling. "All I can say, Sheriff, is that they were charged with misdemeanors that never should have landed them where they are. But I'm just a public defender. You have any idea how thick my case load is? I usually meet my clients for the first time when they're dragged into the court room, shackled, and the only thing I have time for are quick questions about how they want to plead and whether the charges have merit, and then the judge is there.

"Dangerous? I don't know where that came from. All I can tell you is that one of them was a street preacher, the other a veteran. Both, I think, were in the wrong place at the wrong time. In that altercation with a cop, the cop said they were the aggressors. I wish I could tell you more, but I'm sorry to say I don't know anything about them. I had basically five minutes with each of them.

"Oh, here it is. Rafe Jackson was given five years and was up for parole soon. Holter was given a ridiculous sentence of eight years, plus three years' probation over some bullshit. Excuse the French. But he was angry. I understand lack of sleep in jail does that, but he didn't keep his cool in front of the judge, which landed him on his wrong side. The first thing I tell everyone is respect first, because the judge doesn't give a shit about their problems, threats from other inmates, that they can't get a shower, take a shit, or sleep, or that there's some guy inside named Sue who won't leave them be." The lawyer sighed again.

Marcus glanced over to see how intently Suzanne was staring at the cell phone. "So why the shoot to kill order?" he finally asked.

"Honestly, Sheriff?"

"Please. Would be appreciated."

"How often do you hear of prisoners escaping?"

Marcus shook his head. "Rarely, if ever."

"My guess is you're dealing with ego," Wallace said. "A pissed-off warden of a state prison is not someone you want to be on the wrong side of. Can you imagine what would happen to the prisoners if caught alive? Their fates would be worse at the hands of the warden, who basically owns them, and there's no one they can call for help. If that warden wants to, he can make sure a prisoner disappears, never sees the light of day, and everyone knows it, those inside, anyway. My opinion, Sheriff? The shoot to kill may have been a mercy."

Suzanne hissed, and Marcus glanced over to her before saying, "You know anything about a girlfriend or family of either of these two? The warden mentioned something about one of them having a brother up towards Billings and a girlfriend around Livingston."

The man grunted. "Here it is. Tracy Mitchell, girlfriend of Rafe. It just says Livingston. I don't have an address or phone number. You said one of them has a brother? I have nothing here. The only reason I know about the girlfriend is that she's left me a lot of messages, hounding me to file an appeal."

Marcus shook his head. His sister had pulled out her cell phone and was typing something in, then held the screen up toward him.

"Marcus, an address right here for Tracy," she said.

He only nodded. "Okay, thanks, George. If you hear from Rafe or think of anything else, you call me."

"Goodnight, Sheriff," was all the lawyer said.

Marcus hit the end call icon and turned to his sister. "How far is she from here?"

Suzanne tapped her phone, then gestured to the road ahead. "Not far. So does this mean you're not taking me home?"

He pulled in a breath, knowing his sister wanted him to say the one thing he wasn't about to. "Nope, but you'll have to stay in the car this time. Now give me the address and don't let this go to your head."

He turned left on a secondary road just outside of town, still rural, with houses on lots that were an acre or two in size. A lot of places to hide. There was that feeling again. Just how far behind were Sheriff Lester and his men or Kellogg's guards?

"I'm letting nothing go to my head," Suzanne said. "I know my limitations very well, but at the same time, Marcus, I know how to look up an address, I know what a crime scene looks like, and I know when someone shouldn't be someplace. Oh, Tracy Mitchell's place is right here." She gestured to a dirt driveway with a small double-wide and an old pickup parked out front.

Marcus pulled in behind it and parked, then turned to his sister, who had unfastened her seatbelt and already had her hand on the door. "Suzanne, I mean it. This time, I need you to stay here in the car."

She looked over to him in that way of hers, and for a moment, he thought she'd argue. He took in the double-wide. The outside light was off, and the house was dark. In bed? Likely, considering it was well past midnight.

"If you want me to stay here, I will," Suzanne said. "But, Marcus, you're alone. There's still the matter of this prisoner on the loose, and the warden wants him dead. If he's here, you think he's going to come easy? The least I can do is watch your back."

Damn, why did she have to be so reasonable? He

knew he needed to say no. He gave his door a yank. "You stay behind me and out of the way," he said.

Then he stepped out of the vehicle, and so did Suzanne. He closed his door quietly, and she did the same. As he walked around the front of the vehicle, she fell in beside him. She gestured to the door, up some narrow rickety steps, and he nodded.

He pulled the screen door open and gave a solid knock on the wooden door behind it. "Sheriff's department!" he called out, then glanced down to his sister, who stood at the bottom of the steps, looking at him and around. He heard footsteps inside, the outside light flicked on, and his hand went right to his holstered gun as he heard the lock click.

"Tracy Mitchell, open up!" he yelled.

The door cracked open a bit. A light was on inside. The woman standing there was short, with a narrow face, messy brown hair, brown eyes, and a dark blue robe. "Can I help you?"

He didn't think she was that old. Mid-thirties, maybe. "Are you Tracy Mitchell?"

She nodded. "I am. What is this about?"

He looked past her, listening for anything. "There was a prison escape tonight, Rafe Jackson and Holter Donnelly. I understand you know them?"

She pressed her hand to her chest, pulling her robe closed. "I do, but I don't know anything about them escaping. You must be mistaken."

Again, he wondered if she was hiding something. "So you haven't heard from either of them."

She made a face and shrugged. "No, I haven't."

He wondered if she'd tell the truth. "Well, let me put it this way: The warden and the Stillwater County sheriff's office have a shoot to kill order out on both of them, and law enforcement has been alerted they're both considered dangerous. I was just at a crime scene where the body of Holter Donnelly was, shot in the back. So, again, I'm going to ask you about Rafe. You see him? And before you answer me, know that I'm trying to save his life, but he's got to turn himself in, because the law out there are looking for him, and they aren't going to ask questions. They're going to shoot first. You understand what I'm saying?"

She said nothing, just swallowed and licked her lips, nervous. She glanced out to his sister at the bottom of the stairs. "I don't know what I can tell you, Sheriff, but if you're really trying to help, and I hope you are, then you have to know the truth of the matter. Neither of them should have been in jail. The only thing they did wrong was stand before the wrong judge, and that was after a cop lied about what happened. They're not dangerous, neither of them." She sounded pissed.

"Then you won't mind if we come in and have a look around."

She was standing right in the doorway, her arms crossed, both scared and pissed. "You have a warrant? Because unless you do, you're not setting one foot in my house." She moved to shut the door, but Marcus slapped his hand to it before she could.

"I guess you didn't hear me," he said. "Rafe is a wanted man, a criminal, and in the eyes of the law, he's already been convicted. I don't need a warrant, so unless you want to find yourself arrested for obstruction or aiding and abetting a fugitive, a felony conviction for which you'd serve a good many years..."

Her eyes flashed with fury as she stepped back, letting go of the door. Marcus pushed it open, and she just stood there, staring at him with an anger he didn't even know how to reason with.

"Well, don't just stand there," she said. "Come on in. But hear me well, Sheriff: I will not be intimidated, pushed around, or threatened. I already said Rafe isn't here. Just don't make a mess, and don't be long. I have an early day tomorrow." Then she turned her back, walked into the small kitchen, and lifted a kettle and filled it with water.

Marcus stepped into the living room, seeing a large flatscreen, a small green sectional, and piles of papers and books. On one wall, papers and notes were pinned up along with photos of a cop and a judge, as well as a timeline. He found himself looking back to the woman, who was now watching him.

"What's this?" He gestured to the wall, on which there was also a copy of a police report.

"What does it look like?" Tracy said. "I told you Rafe and Holter didn't deserve what happened. Their only crime was standing up to a bully for those who couldn't stand up for themselves. But as you said, Sheriff, he's been convicted. To hell with whether it was right." She put the kettle on the stove and flicked on the burner.

"I never said that," Marcus said. "Right now, I'm just trying to prevent Rafe from also ending up on a slab in the morgue. If he's innocent, I promise you I'll look into it, but I've got to find him first." He knew he sounded reasonable. He heard the squeak of the floor and turned to see his sister in the doorway.

Tracy shut her eyes for a second. He wondered if this was where she would come clean. She had to know something. Then she flicked her eyes open and gave her head a shake. "As I said, Sheriff, I haven't heard from him, so if you don't mind, have your look-see, and then, with all due respect, get the fuck out of my house."

CHAPTER 5

Time was ticking. Marcus pulled open the driver's door of his cruiser, then slid behind the wheel. Suzanne was still just inside the house, talking with Tracy.

He had searched the two bedrooms, two bathrooms, and small laundry room but knew no one was hiding inside. He still figured Tracy knew something, though, and he didn't have a clue how his sister managed to talk to a woman who'd basically told him to go fuck himself. Tracy was gesturing passionately now, maybe because Suzanne wasn't wearing a badge, carrying a gun, or representing a system that had incarcerated someone she cared about. Or maybe it was because Suzanne was less of a threat.

"You still there, Marcus?" Harold said. He had called a few seconds ago and was waiting on the line.

"Yeah. Tell me you have something, anything, on Jackson and Donnelly," Marcus said. "The lawyer said one was a street preacher and the other a veteran. I'm at

Tracy Mitchell's right now, and she's less than forthcoming. Suzanne is talking to her."

"My wife, Suzanne?" Harold said rather sharply.

"Yes, your wife, my sister—who, evidently, Tracy likes better than me. She's fine. Just don't tell her she was helpful tonight."

Harold made a rude sound on the other end. "Whatever. We'll save that discussion for another time. About the two prisoners, they were friends. Rafe Jackson was a retired veteran, served in Afghanistan. He took the BUD/S training but washed out the first week, and apparently, that was it for him in the military. Donnelly was a minister who worked mostly with the homeless, vets, the down and out, anyone on the street. So he knew the streets and who was there, but he had a problem with the local authorities and butted heads with them all the time.

"He'd been issued numerous parking tickets, which I guarantee was because he pissed off the wrong person, or many of them, and they had him in their line of sight. He was fined for trespassing and mischief, but never anything more than a fine, so I'm having a hard time understanding what happened to escalate things to him standing before a judge, arrested. There was a charge of inciting violence, but that disappeared off the books. There were verbal threats to a cop, but not sure what was said. This is the first time I've seen just the charge with no explanation of what, why, and how.

"As for assault of a police officer, from what I've read, a cop sprayed gas over a homeless guy from his car, and either Jackson or Donnelly threw an umbrella at the cop's car. A statement was filed by Donnelly about the cop, but I can't find it anywhere. This was some cop over in Billings. He arrested him, and I'm not sure how all this had them before a judge and sentenced with what they were. As for them being dangerous..."

Harold paused. "Let's see. They fed the homeless, tried to find shelter for those on the street, and were basically do-gooders who gave a shit and tried to help people no one would help. The shoot to kill order, I can find no reason for that at all. If something happened in the prison, I've got nothing here. You said they shot Donnelly? He was the preacher. Wow, something is wrong there. Jackson grew up in a small town, Shelby, over in Toole County, hunting, fishing, tracking. He'd know how to hide and stay hidden. Donnelly had a brother-in-law outside Billings, Jack Cooper, but I've got nothing here on a sister. I can send you the address, or do you want me to head out?"

Marcus took in Suzanne, who was gesturing to him from the open doorway. What the hell was she up to now? "I'm still here at Tracy's," he said. "Looks like I'm headed back inside to have a word, maybe. Your wife is waving me back. Why don't you give the brother-in-law a call? I wouldn't be surprised if he hasn't already been called by the warden, or Sheriff Lester, or the Yellowstone County sheriff. But yes, call him, and let me know what he says. So no other family, friends? You said Donnelly was a minister. I think he pissed off the wrong person. From his face, someone had worked him over. Not recent. The bruising, from what I saw, was old. See if you can find out anything from inside the prison. Damn,

I just have a feeling Tracy knows something. I mean, think about it. If you were in trouble and on the run, wouldn't you go to Suzanne, or at least call and let her know you were okay?"

Harold grunted. "One, that would never be me. Right now, the best thing for me and Suzanne is for you to talk some sense into her. She's got a baby. You do know what this is about with her?"

Marcus pulled in a breath and stepped out of the cruiser. He nodded to his sister, who gestured sharply and made a face as if he were taking too long. "Yeah, I know," he said. "I'll talk to her." He let out a sigh.

"You do that," Harold said. "I'll call you and let you know what I come up with." Then he hung up, and Marcus pocketed his phone, closed his door, and started back to the double-wide and up the rickety steps.

"Tracy, tell Marcus what you just told me about Holter," Suzanne said as Marcus stepped inside.

Tracy was pouring a steaming mug of tea, and she gestured to Suzanne and said, "Cream or sugar?"

Suzanne walked over to the counter and reached for the mug. "No, this is fine. Thanks so much, Tracy. You really have done a lot of work here, your research. How long had Holter been ministering on the streets?"

Marcus knew he was frowning. It was the middle of the night, and his sister had a woman who'd basically told him to fuck off making her tea. He wanted to give his head a shake. Tracy lifted another steaming mug, standing on the other side of the small counter. She dragged her gaze over to Marcus, and he swore daggers appeared again in her eyes.

"Ministering was Holter's life," she said. "He'd been doing it for twenty years, started as a kid. Spent time in Panama, in Africa, at a church in Columbia Falls, over in Wyoming, and then in Billings. With everything going on, when the housing market fell and so many lost their homes, he was out there, helping where he could. He said most ministers want to preach to people who can pay. He said a lot have sold their souls and forgotten what it's really about, helping those who need it, not those who can pay for it.

"In doing so, he had a knack for pissing off the wrong people. He called a spade a spade and challenged anyone who took advantage of the little guy. He was as politically incorrect as they come. He considered himself an activist, saying too many believe freedom is not something you really have to fight for. He believed our freedom was being snatched away every day by politicians and corporations who were all about profit. I think it was six years ago when Rafe got back, left the military, and went through a hard time. It was Holter who pulled him up, said he needed him to watch his back. Holter was a born warrior.

"Rafe turned him down, but when Holter was beat up and dumped in an alley, Rafe was there. Long story. After that, Rafe made sure no one messed with Holter. He watched his back. Said there were cops and business owners who wanted Holter gone and brought him a heap of trouble. Can you imagine, you're just trying to help those who have nothing, nowhere to go, and then one day you lose it? Let me be clear, Holter had a temper, but if you saw how some of those cops, community leaders, and business owners treated the people he was trying to help, you'd be angry too.

"To be clear, it's not all cops, but it takes only one or two. The brotherhood protects the ones who kick the shit out of innocent people. There was an elderly woman with a walker on the streets, and one day a cop took her walker and dumped it in a trash bin. Rafe filed a complaint with the county sheriff's office in Billings. It wasn't just one thing, either. One cop took a shopping cart filled with all a man's belongings. It was endless, the beatdowns, and everyone on the street was scared to point a finger.

"The gaslighting by the media was the worst, he said. He saw a story about a vagrant urinating at the back door of some big store, and it said the resulting confrontation turned ugly. The business owner was on the news, complaining about the homeless in the area, who were defecating all over and had damaged his property, trying to break in, stealing, threatening customers. Except it wasn't true. The media put a few crisis actors there to say it had happened. Rafe said the shop owner didn't want the homeless there, so he made up a story, created a lie. The people believed the news, and no one questioned it."

Marcus glanced over to the clock, feeling the lateness, wondering where this was going. "You know, Tracy, I sympathize, I really do," he said. "But how is this helping us find Rafe? So he watched Holter's back, and now he's on the run. Holter is dead. Someone worked him over in jail, and I'm afraid Rafe is next unless you level with me."

Suzanne put down her mug. Tracy lifted her chin and glanced away.

"You know where he is, don't you?" Marcus said.

Outside, an engine started.

Marcus ran to the door and slammed his hand on the screen to open it just as the pickup floored it and backed out around his car. He glanced back to Tracy and saw it written all over her face. "He was here the whole time," he snapped.

Tracy had put down her tea, fear in her eyes.

Marcus pulled his cuffs from his pouch as he strode to her. "Turn around," he said, then slapped the cuffs on her and grabbed her arm. Suzanne was looking at him with wide eyes, and he said, "You stay here with her. Call Therese and tell her to get over here and pick her up."

He ran to the door, and as he yanked it open, he heard Tracy yelling, "You'll never find him!"

"Marcus, I swear I didn't know," Suzanne called out.

He just shook his head, still hearing the squeal of the truck as it reached the road. He sprinted out to his cruiser, started it, and gave it gas, spinning the car around and flooring it down the driveway. He hit all the ruts, following the trail of dust to another road that led farther from town. He drove faster than he ever had, his high-beams just reaching the back end of an old white pickup rounding the bend ahead.

CHAPTER 6

M arcus had lost him.

"Fuck!" He slapped his steering wheel, stopped on the side of the dark, narrow highway. A river flowed in the canyon below, and he was surrounded by forested hills and mountains. He didn't know which pullout or trail to try next, as they all went off into the middle of nowhere. If he had the wrong vehicle, he could drive miles down a trail and never find Rafe. He needed eyes, help, something.

"Sheriff, are you there?" Therese said over the radio.

He reached for it. "Tell me you're on your way over to Tracy Mitchell's. I left her cuffed with my sister. Rafe got away. He's in an old early eighties Ford pickup, off white. Didn't get the plate number. I need you to run that model under Tracy Mitchell and see what you can find." He'd bit out the last part, pressing his hand to his forehead and jamming his fingers through his short, wavy hair.

"Will do. I'll run that for you, but Harold told me to

stay put at the station. He's on his way or should be there now. The phones here are blowing up. Some of the locals don't sleep and called to wake everyone else up about a prison escape, a dangerous criminal. The notice came from Stillwater County to ours. The last five callers have demanded to know what their tax dollars are paying for if Stillwater is looking after them for us. They want to know where the hell you are and why you're not letting anyone know about the fugitives. I could go on, but I think you get it. Then the mayor called."

"Fuck," he said again under his breath, feeling the anger pulse. The radio clicked into silence. He'd dragged Suzanne out with him to the crime scene because he hadn't been given all the details, but now he realized his mistake. He should have put out a notice first. The pieces were stacking against him.

"Just say we're working on it and I'm out looking," he said. "Tell the mayor or anyone else that I don't have time for handholding or questions because I'm fucking busy doing my job. Just tell them the situation is handled." But it wasn't handled, and he was so done with everyone questioning what he did. "Just do your best. You by any chance get a heads-up from Stillwater County that they were sending out an alert?" he asked, though he already knew the answer.

"No," she said. "Popped up on my phone, and then the first call came in. There's a statewide warrant for a dangerous offender and a warning to the residents. I can read it off to you."

He tapped on his cell phone and saw the text alert in his notifications along with a photo of the man he was tracking. Yeah, they really were pulling out all the stops: Possibly armed and dangerous. Shoot to kill. Lock your doors.

"No, I have it here," he said. "Look, I lost Rafe Jackson. I'm on Highway 89 and lost him just past River Road. Going to need some help out here. I'm going to head back to Tracy Mitchell's and have a word with her again before Harold hauls her out of there. Let me know if there's anything else."

The last things he wanted to deal with were politics and soothing ruffled feathers. He hung up the radio, put the car in gear, and wheeled back around on the empty darkened highway to drive back to Tracy's.

He pulled in fifteen minutes later just as Harold was walking a handcuffed Tracy to his cruiser in her bathrobe. Suzanne was following him, the light from the trailer spilling out behind her. Harold held the back door of his cruiser open, his hand on Tracy's head to help her into the uncomfortable back seat, with bars and no leg room.

Marcus parked behind the cruiser and stepped out, taking in his deputy, who wore blue jeans and a red t-shirt, out of uniform, with just his holstered gun. Harold just leaned against the car as Marcus approached and glanced in to Tracy, who wore sneakers and was glaring daggers up at him.

"He got away," Marcus said. "There were half a dozen pullouts, trails, and backroads he could have taken, if not more." He looked back to Harold. "You read her her rights?"

Suzanne was standing just off to the side, and Harold

glanced back to her. Something about the motion told Marcus the two of them had exchanged words. The tension was thick in the air.

Harold flicked his hand toward Tracy, still leaning against the car. "Yeah, she's been read," he said, then gestured toward Suzanne, who had stepped closer. "You want to tell Marcus what you two were talking about when I got here?"

This shitshow was turning into something else. Marcus let his gaze settle back on his sister as he said, "Suzanne, you're not a cop. What the hell are you doing?" He motioned for her to move away from the car, far enough away that it was just them, out of hearing of Tracy and Harold. Taking in her wide eyes, he was starting to feel like a brother coming between husband and wife.

"Marcus, just hear me out," she said. "Look, I've never seen you so angry, and I feel like shit. I had no idea she was playing me. I really believed she didn't know where he was. He was hiding right here the whole time. I felt gut-punched even though I don't know her."

He didn't have time for this. He let out a sigh of frustration.

"She said she was sorry," Suzanne said.

He angled his head, really looking at his sister. "Bullshit. She's only sorry she got caught lying to a cop, aiding and abetting, harboring a criminal. Just to start, she's looking at a lot of time. That's the only fucking reason she's sorry." Damn, he was pissed. He really hated being played.

"No, Marcus, you're wrong," Suzanne said. She shut

her eyes and shook her head, flustered. "Wait, I meant to say you're right about part of it, but she knew he wouldn't be given a fair shake, and she didn't trust you. She figured you'd shoot him down just like Holter Donnelly. Can't blame her, because she doesn't know you, Marcus. I told her you'd never do that. She said she's just waiting for something to happen to her now, too. She said Holter turned himself in so Rafe could get away. Rafe was furious. Holter had been hurt. His leg was buggered, fell or something, twisted it. Rafe was practically carrying him, helping him walk, but they heard the dogs gaining on them.

"The manhunt was closing in on their trail, and Holter told him to leave him. Rafe didn't want to. He said no, but Holter just went out into the flashlights and yelled, raising his hands up and surrendering to give Rafe time to get away. Rafe started running but circled back when he heard a gunshot, and he spotted Holter on the ground, his hands cuffed behind his back. He said the guards and cops staged the scene. They fucking murdered him, Marcus. That's what she said. So I understand what she did. You have to understand she didn't know you wouldn't do the same thing. I would probably have done the same in her shoes."

He stared at his sister, who was imploring him. "You sure she said he was cuffed?"

Suzanne winced and shook her head. "I don't know how you do this job, Marcus. Yeah, she said he was cuffed. It's possible, isn't it?"

"What, that cops shot a man in handcuffs in the back, like an execution? I can't believe that, even of

Lonnie and Sheriff Lester. I have no love lost for them, but that's just way beyond…" Heaviness had settled in thick around them. He knew stuff like that happened, but not with those he knew.

"I think I'll have Harold take me home after this, if that's okay," Suzanne said. "I just want to hold Arnie."

He glanced over to a waiting Harold and Tracy, who wouldn't look at him from the back seat, then dragged his gaze back to his sister. He squeezed her shoulder, then turned back to Harold and the cruiser.

"Suzanne is going to have you take her home," he said, and Harold nodded but didn't move. "Tracy, is it true Holter was cuffed and shot in the back, that he turned himself in? Did Rafe really see that happen, see him shot and cuffed on the ground? No bullshit. I won't stand for any more lies."

The inside light was on. Tracy's brown hair was still messy from bed. The way she stared up at him, he didn't think she'd answer him, but she said, "Rafe wouldn't lie. He's as good and honest and decent as they come. He heard the shot and doubled back, and he knew what they'd done."

How many times had he heard a story like that from someone he'd arrested, someone he'd questioned, from family members or girlfriends who believed the lies they had been told?

"Tell me where Rafe went," he said. "Do you know? It'll be easier on you."

"You think I give a shit about that? You're going to lock me up, put me before some corrupt judge, and make sure I get no deals, no break. You think I don't know that?

You think I didn't watch on the sidelines when even the public defender assigned to Holter and Rafe didn't bother to untwist the bullshit? Their misdemeanors deserved a ticket and fine, at worst, but the judge sentenced them for the other bullshit they added, which wasn't even true. Those two should never have been arrested, let alone given jail time, but the word of some cowardly crooked cop was worth more than theirs.

"Your sister did her best to sell me on you, but if you're so good and decent, Sheriff O'Connell, why are you not looking into what happened to them in jail or out there? Your sister said you were at the crime scene, saw Holter shot up, dead, yet here you are. Let me ask you this: The cop who shot Holter, will your next call be to him so you all make sure you get Rafe next? Even I know dead men can't talk."

The way she said it, he suspected she was more afraid than she was letting on. There was strong, and there was stupid, but something about her conviction told him she really did believe whatever she'd been told.

He leaned down and reached for her arm. "Come on, get out."

"What? No, what are you doing?" Her voice rose sharply as he pulled her out of the back of the vehicle.

"Marcus, what are you doing?" Harold said in a low voice.

Marcus pulled his keys from his pocket and undid one handcuff and then the other, freeing her hands. Her hand went right to her wrist, and her wide eyes stared back at him in shock and surprise, unable now to hide how scared she was.

"Okay, Tracy," he said. "I want the damn truth. I get that you think Rafe is being honest with you, but the only people who really know what happened out there are not here. You think you know what happened, but everything you're saying means nothing. It's hearsay. No investigation is going to happen because the girlfriend of a convicted criminal who escaped from prison said someone in law enforcement tried to hurt him or shot someone in handcuffs in the back. You won't be believed. I'm not saying you're lying, but you're trusting someone who has no rights. He's a convicted criminal on the run. No one has explained to me why he's considered dangerous or why a shoot to kill order was issued, but that doesn't mean a cop can kill a man who has surrendered and is cuffed. So how about you explain to me what the fuck is really going on here? No bullshit." Even he could hear how short and on edge he sounded.

She licked her lips and took a shallow breath. "How can I trust you?" Her voice caught.

"Where I'm standing, I don't see that you have a whole lot of fucking choices."

She shut her eyes and pulled her arms over her chest, then nodded. "And then you'll let me go?"

Marcus shook his head. "No, but I promise you, and you have my word on it, that I'll make sure you're given a fair shake."

CHAPTER 7

His sister was over by the door inside the double-wide, talking to Harold, but what she was saying, Marcus couldn't make out. He turned back to Tracy, who was now sitting at the small kitchen table in an old wooden chair, her hands linked together in front of her. Her purple nightgown peeked out from her housecoat.

"Rafe is a really good, decent man," she said. "He has a conscience and at times a temper when he sees injustice. He's never been able to turn his back on anyone being taken advantage of or hurt. Anyone else would mind their own business, but he steps in. I told him too many times that it wasn't healthy for him, that sometimes he needed to look away, that some fights weren't his, but he didn't want to hear it. I loved him and hated him at the same time for being that way.

"He wasn't always like that. He changed so much after his time in Afghanistan. I was told to expect it, told men never return the same. Some are so fucked up in the head that they're never right again. War does that—what they see, what they do, so many secrets they have to keep and want to keep. When Rafe came back, he said his life before meant nothing. He saw things he'd never talk about, but I'd see the cold sweat come over him when he got it stuck in his head."

Marcus had his phone out, recording. He waited for her to tell him to turn it off, but she didn't.

She glanced down to the phone and then back up to him. "We've been together off and on over ten years. He asked me to marry him when he came back on leave the first time, and I said yes, but then something changed. He never gave me a ring, and he never brought it up again. It was as if he didn't remember asking, or he'd changed his mind. I never asked."

Marcus flicked his gaze to the clock on the wall. It was now just past two in the morning, and he knew sleep wouldn't be coming anytime soon. This would be a long night. "You know, Tracy, I'm sorry about this, but there are a lot of stories like Rafe's. Where is he? You have to know where he went. You gave him the keys to your pickup."

"The truck is his, not mine. Look, Rafe is a good man. When he and Holter met, Rafe said that was the first time he was doing something that gave him a reason to get out of bed. I'm telling you this, Sheriff, so you understand that the picture being painted isn't him." She flattened one hand on the table in front of him as if willing him to see things her way. "You see, I never had the courage to ask him to leave, but I was working my way up to it when he went to Billings. He got a call from an army buddy about a vet from their unit who had fallen off the radar. They found him living on the streets, messed up, fucked up, at rock bottom. I know he and a few of his army buddies got him off the street, got him cleaned up, found him some help and a place to stay. That was where he met Holter. Not the kind of minister I would've expected. He didn't have a church, didn't want a fancy building. He spent his time on the streets every day, checking on the people who lived there. 'Giving hope to people who saw none,' was what Rafe said. Holter helped with Rafe's friend, and after that..." She lifted her hand and let out a sigh.

"So was that how they started working together, then?"

She shrugged and glanced at Suzanne and Harold, who were still by the door. Harold had turned from her and was headed over, the floor squeaking with each step. Suzanne hadn't moved.

"Excuse me, Marcus," Harold said, gesturing to him.

Marcus knew he wanted a word, so he stood up, leaving Tracy at the table. "What?"

"I called Ryan. He's going to come out and pick up Suzanne, since I left Tessa and Owen's compact at the station. But who knows the parks better than Ryan? You know what I'm saying?"

Marcus glanced over at his sister. Her expression was that of a kicked puppy, one he couldn't remember seeing before. He only nodded. Ryan had always been his go-to for anything in the park, on the trails, because moni-toring the parks was what he did.

Marcus said nothing as he walked over to Suzanne. Her eyes were puffy and red rimmed, and she couldn't hide that she'd shed a few tears. He winced, wondering whether he should look away and save her dignity. "Don't beat yourself up," he said. "This is an impossible situation."

She pulled the back of her hand over her nose, wiping it, and sniffed. "I know, I get that. I'm sorry if I screwed up here in any way. I was just trying to help, to show you that…" She didn't look at him, and damn, he felt like a bastard.

"Hey, I get it," he said. "Sometimes, when you're new on the job, you come in with naivete, believing you're doing the right thing. Every one of us has believed someone who lied right to our faces, but we thought we had that magic touch. I've been doing this a long time, Suzanne. You just get a nose for when someone is lying, hiding something, or if a crime scene is too neat and tidy. If this makes you feel any better, you helped."

The way her eyes widened, he realized she was taking it the wrong way.

"Don't get any ideas," he said. "Go home to your son when Ryan gets here." He pulled in a breath. When she tried to force a smile, he let out a weary sigh. "I'm going to regret saying this, but after I find this guy, hopefully before anyone else, we'll talk, and maybe I can find you something at the station."

She threw her arms around him.

"I said maybe," he added.

"Oh, Marcus, thank you…" She stepped back and slapped his arm, beaming.

He glanced over at Harold, who was talking to Tracy, before dragging his gaze back to Suzanne, breathing in the old smell of the trailer. "You make sure Harold is okay with it first. That's on you, because I don't want him pissed at me. You get him on board, understand?"

She lifted her hands, and he turned away, knowing he'd made her night. He walked back over to Harold and Tracy and just angled his head. By the way Harold looked at him, he suspected he already knew, but he said nothing as he walked away, back over to Suzanne, and Marcus sat back down in the chair.

"You're a good brother," Tracy said. She gestured toward Suzanne.

Marcus didn't pull his gaze from her. There was no way he was talking about his family with anyone. He had to remember where he was. "Let's get back to it," he said. "You said Rafe and Holter met over Rafe's friend on the streets? So they didn't know each other before that?"

Tracy shook her head. "Rafe just kind of started showing up to help Holter, watch his back. He said at least he could do something he was good at there, after seeing everything Holter did for the community, which he received very little support for. He said Holter had a target on him. He was really good at making enemies of the kinds of people who should've been doing what he was doing—cops, business owners, institutions and programs that we pay for, but the money never seems to go where it's needed.

"Rafe was good at keeping an eye out, seeing where

trouble was. More than that, he could tell when Holter was walking right into danger, which he did too many times, as if he didn't have a clue about self-preservation. He was selfless, kind, generous. Maybe that was why I tried not to like him. But he didn't care what people thought. You ever met a warrior, someone who has a fight inside him, deep down? Well, that was Holter.

"He pushed it. He was arrested a few times, and new bylaws suddenly came into force that no one knew about. He was fined for trespassing once, for creating a disturbance, always going head to head with authority. I warned Rafe, but he wouldn't listen. I never found out about the last arrest until Rafe was in jail too. We couldn't afford a lawyer, and the public defender was a pitiful excuse for one. They landed before a judge who hated them. I swear he'd been given marching orders. The entire thing was a farce.

"Rafe's only crime was standing up to cops who were acting as front men to someone else. I never would have believed it could happen, but it did. They were arrested, and what went on inside the jail was bad. Rafe didn't say much, but he did say Holter still had a target on him in there. He was tossed in solitary, always had fresh bruising on him…"

It was a sad story, but nothing relevant. Marcus rested his arm on the table and turned off the recording, and Tracy's brow knit in confusion.

"I appreciate the backstory," he said. "It helps. It sounds like they were railroaded, but unfortunately, Tracy, one of them is now dead. You said Holter gave himself up to save Rafe? Well, there will be no justice for Holter if Rafe is dead too. You understand what I'm saying? There's a manhunt out there. The prison guards, police from another county, and the marshals will all have been called in, and it's going to grow. They'll put choppers up, more dogs out. You need to tell me where Rafe is, where he went. And don't tell me you don't know. Out of everyone, I believe you do. He came here to you because he trusts you. I'm trying to save his life, Tracy."

She shut her eyes. He knew he was reaching her in some way. He hoped he was, at least. When she looked up at him, he saw vulnerability in those blue eyes—and a fighting spirit that hadn't been broken.

"Tracy, I give you my word I'll bring him in alive, but he's out of options. If it happened the way you said, then he's got a target on him too, and the only win here is me catching him so the truth can come out. There's a small window now. Once they know he's still alive, they'll come for him, and they'll shut him down, shut him up, and bury him. You and I both know that if he goes back to prison, he'll never be seen or heard from again unless the truth is out there, unless his story is out."

"And you're saying it can only be you who brings him in. What are you going to do, Sheriff, arrest him, get him to talk? Because I guarantee you may not be given the chance to talk to him."

He heard a car outside and turned to see headlights flashing through the window. "You're right. Time isn't on my side, which is why the longer we sit here with you not telling me where to find him, the more his chances of coming out of this alive slip away."

"I don't trust you." She pulled her arms over her chest and leaned back. Her mouth firmed, and her eyes went hard again.

"I get that, but we don't have the luxury of sitting here so I can convince you. I'm telling you my word means something, and his best shot is me. Deep down, I think you know that."

She pressed both hands to her face. As he heard the door open, she fisted her hands and swore under her breath. "Fine, but you'll have to take me with you."

There was no way. He moved to stand. "Not happening."

"Seems to me you're asking me to trust you, but you won't do the same. You show up without me and Rafe will never believe you're on his side. If you really want to help, you really want to save his life, then you take me, because he'll listen only to me."

Ryan had stepped inside. Marcus turned to his brother, his brown hair messy, wearing blue jeans and a navy hoodie over a wrinkled t-shirt. He knew Rafe could be anywhere.

"Fine," he said. "But I swear to you, Tracy, this is your last chance. You fuck me around or I find out you're lying to me, leading me on a wild goose chase, I'll bury you. I'm a fair man, but I mean what I say."

She gave a nod. "Same to you, Sheriff," was all she said. She stood up. "Give me five minutes to pull some clothes on."

He looked over to his brother, his sister, and Harold,

then gestured to the hall. "You have one minute and not a second more."

As he watched her hurry down the hall to the bedroom on the end, he just hoped he wasn't also making the rookie mistake of trusting someone who couldn't be trusted.

CHAPTER 8

"You doing okay back there, Tracy?" Ryan said from the passenger seat. An assault rifle was mounted between him and Marcus, and wire mesh and bars separated them from the back, where Tracy sat. She now wore a brown sweater over blue jeans, and she'd run a brush through her hair.

"Well, considering I'm not cuffed or on my way to jail, sure, I'm great," she said. "Your sister going to be okay? She seems rather nice. And your deputy is your brother-in-law? Sheriff, your family seems to run the law here."

Marcus squeezed the steering wheel, knowing Tracy had shown a lot of interest in Suzanne and Harold, who had driven out ahead of them. He knew she was digging, but he wasn't sharing. He gave the car more gas and flicked his brights on, heading back down the darkened highway to where he'd lost sight of Rafe Jackson.

Ryan said nothing. Maybe he knew to be careful, and

the fact was that none of them shared family business with anyone they didn't know.

"My sister's fine," Marcus said. "Let's talk about this land of Rafe's. You said it's in his father's name." He flicked his gaze to the radio, feeling a weight on his shoulders. After bringing Suzanne home, Harold would go to the station, where he could man what Marcus suspected was a shitload of trouble coming at them. The politics with this job would be his undoing.

"Mm-hmm," was all Tracy said.

Marcus flicked his gaze back to her in the rear-view mirror. She was looking out the side window. "You said there's a cabin on the property, a mile off the road?"

"No, I said he was building a cabin, or he planned to. He bought most of the lumber, and it's been tarped and sitting there for years."

Ryan was looking back at Tracy too. "I know where that is," he said. "It's been sitting there a long time."

She sighed. "Yeah, life got in the way. It was more than five years ago that he bought the wood, the designs, then tarped it and left it. I stopped asking him when he stopped hearing me, stopped answering me."

Ryan glanced over to Marcus in the darkened car. "Fire hazard," he said in a low voice. "Stumbled across it a while ago. If I remember, the road in isn't easy to find. You'll need a four by four in some places."

Marcus rounded the bend, coming up on where he'd lost Rafe, seeing flashing lights, emergency services, and damn cops blocking the road. "What the fuck is this?" he snapped, pressing the brakes and rolling to a stop in front of an approaching cop, state police, carrying a flashlight. He rolled his window down and didn't recognize the young lady in uniform. "What's going on here?" he asked.

"Escaped prisoner," she said. "Sheriff Lester has a search party out, and the prisons called everyone in. There's a grid search happening, with dogs, and they've called in a chopper, I understand, from Boise. You need to get through?"

Marcus just stared. He knew she was looking into the car at Ryan and then at Tracy in the back. He flicked his gaze to her nametag. "Trooper Welch, is it?"

She nodded. "Yes, sir."

Marcus put the car in park. "You know who I am?"

She frowned and stepped back, shining her flashlight on his door. "Sheriff…"

"Sheriff O'Connell of Livingston, Park County. You know where you're standing right now?"

She paused.

"Let me help you out," he said. "You're in my county. So who the fuck ordered this without contacting me? You can't be so new to the job that you don't understand who you're first call is to. In my county, nothing happens without me knowing it. Now who's in charge here?"

Evidently, she was smart enough to realize her mistake. "Sheriff Lester," she said. "Sorry, Sheriff O'Connell. I only go where they tell me."

"Where is he?"

She stepped back and pointed, then leaned down to him, speaking through the window. "Just drive around my cruiser there," she said. "He's just behind with the flashing lights. They're stopping traffic on both sides, but

I know their focus was just past River Road. Apparently, that's the last sighting. I know there's a report of a pickup."

"Off white, older-model Ford, early eighties," he said, then took in her surprise as she leaned down again.

"Yeah, that's it. All I heard was that the last sighting was around here. Oh, there's Sheriff Lester now."

Marcus looked out to see the sheriff walking his way, flashlight in hand. From the voices in the night, he figured there were dozens out there, looking. He pulled open his door after a glance back to the wide eyes of Tracy and over to Ryan, who he knew was quietly taking everything in. "I'll be right back," he said. "You two stay here."

He stepped out and closed the door, then headed over to the sheriff, who was still wearing his coat and ball cap, walking as if he could do whatever he wanted.

"Now, before you start in about how this is your county," Sheriff Lester said, "you already know that a prison break and escaped prisoner trumps jurisdiction. Told you we have this handled, or we will soon, and then we'll be out of here." He looked around Marcus to his car and jutted his chin toward it. "Who've you got with you?"

Marcus didn't pull his gaze from the sheriff as he pulled his arms over his chest. "Someone who knows the area," he said.

The sheriff was still looking around him. "What about the Mitchell woman, Tracy Mitchell? That her?"

Why did it seem he knew way too much about what Marcus was doing?

"It is," Marcus said.

The sheriff gestured to the car, and Marcus heard the door open behind him.

"What are you doing?" he snapped, turning to see the trooper opening the back door and saying something to Tracy. She reached in the backseat and was pulling her out, and Ryan was out of the car, looking to him, likely wondering what the hell was going on.

"Oh, we'll be taking her," Lester said. "She has a lot to answer for. What was it, hiding an escaped convict?"

Marcus was already walking away, back to the trooper, who had Tracy turned and was cuffing her. Tracy was arguing, her voice pitched high.

"Take those off of her right now!" he ordered, closing the distance. The Trooper had a hand on Tracy's arm, and Tracy had the look of a woman betrayed. "What are you doing?" he yelled.

"Just following orders," the trooper said.

"She's under arrest," Lester said. "This is out of your hands, Marcus. Trooper Welch, you take her and put her in my car. Got some questions for you, Ms. Mitchell, about the pickup Jackson took from your place."

That sinking feeling came out of nowhere again as Lester walked right over to Tracy, who was willing Marcus to do something.

"You know where Rafe Jackson is, don't you, Tracy?" Sheriff Lester called out.

Marcus stopped in front of the trooper, glancing back once to see another cop heading his way. From the Marshals Service, he figured, based on the star badge on a chain around his neck and the vest he wore.

"She knows nothing," Marcus said. "I have no idea where you're getting this from." He put a hand on Tracy's arm.

"Don't you?" the old sheriff said. He pulled his phone out and lifted it in the air, and Marcus heard a recording of him on the radio with Therese. For a second, he felt the ground soften. Everything he'd said was right there: information about the pickup and where he'd lost it, and his fury with Tracy because she had lied to him. Never in a million years would he have ever guessed something like this could happen to him. They had recorded his conversation over the radio with one of his deputies.

He leaned down close to Tracy's ear and said, "Ask for a lawyer. Say nothing." Then he walked back to his car, pulled the front door open, and gave the back door, which was still wide open, a shove closed.

"Hey, Marcus, if you hear anything about where Jackson is, you let us know," the sheriff said.

Marcus said nothing. The marshal had taken a handcuffed Tracy from the trooper. Marcus climbed into his car, and Ryan followed, then reached over to the radio and turned it off.

"What the hell was that?" he said.

Marcus just watched, seeing Tracy being led away to the flashing lights of the other cop cars. She glanced back once, and Marcus could see how badly this was going.

"I'd say they were listening on the radio," he said. "Someone recorded me talking with Therese. It's not as if the channel was private, but they were deliberately watching and listening to everything I did. They knew everything about where I lost Rafe and the pickup, and about Tracy, because I told Therese to dig into her details and come and pick her up after I left her cuffed with Suzanne. They have all of it, and who's to say they don't already know about the land?"

There was no way they were getting through. All he could picture was a man with a bullet in his back and another who would share the same fate.

"Back up and turn around," Ryan said. "Head back about half a mile."

Marcus dragged his gaze over to his brother. "Why?"

"You questioning me? You know I know every nook and cranny and hidey-hole out here. I know every trail, and I know where this property of Rafe's is." Ryan reached for his seatbelt and pulled it on.

Marcus shoved the car in gear and gave it a lot of gas as he backed up and swung around. His brother was watching the side of the road as if he had a sixth sense for everything out there, but then, this was what Ryan did.

"So why are we backtracking?" Marcus said.

Ryan gestured ahead of them. "Because," he said, "I know the back way in."

CHAPTER 9

Driving down what was basically a trail, Marcus heard the chopper before he felt the vibration. It was flying close, he knew, and spotted its lights overhead.

"Keep to the right," Ryan said. "Damn, we really should have brought my pickup. There are a lot of ruts out here." He had his window down and was looking out. "We're close, but just a heads-up: Cell service up here is spotty, nonexistent in places."

Marcus wondered if he'd ever been down this way, maybe when he was a kid. Ryan spent his days in the forests and knew every nook and cranny like the back of his hand. Ryan's cell phone buzzed.

"Just pull over here," Ryan said, flicking his hand at the road. Marcus stopped in the middle of the trail, and Ryan stared at his phone and said, "Wow, it's the Park Service. Three guesses as to whether we've been called in to help with the search."

Marcus nodded at the road. "And they know you're with me?"

Ryan put the phone to his ear. "Hello?" he said. "Uh-huh."

Marcus could make out a male voice on the other end.

"Already know," Ryan said. "Yup, with Marcus. Already out looking. You want to know where we are, exactly?" He was looking right at Marcus now. "South of Livingston. Just had a feeling to look off 540 in Rock Canyon…"

Marcus raised a brow, watching his brother, who was lying through his teeth. Who he was talking to, he didn't know.

"Yup, will let you know what I find," Ryan said, then hung up and held up his phone. "You know if they're tracking us, they know I'm lying. What has Luke said? If you don't want to be tracked, leave your phone at home, use a Faraday bag, or take the SIM card and battery out. How closely do you think they're watching you?"

Marcus shook his head. "With a microscope, considering everything. What's worse, I have no fucking idea what this is really about. Yeah, I get the prison escape. Two cons on the loose, you spare no resources, but the story was too convenient, with too many holes. They can track us by our phones, but that kind of technology isn't used by locals. So where do we go from here?" He turned off the car, and Ryan opened his door, letting his gaze linger on Marcus.

"On foot," he said. "About a mile, not far. You got gear for us? And have you thought about when we get close? He's not going to be just sitting there, waiting for us."

Marcus gave his door a yank and reached for his cell phone mounted on the dash. The radio was still off, and he knew Harold had no idea where he was or what they were doing.

"Bet you wish Luke were here right now," Ryan said as he climbed out.

Marcus followed, pressing the button that opened the trunk, and headed around to survey its contents: a blanket, a medical kit, flares, extra bottled water, batteries, ammunition, a fire extinguisher, and traffic cones he'd never used. "No, I'm glad you're here," he said. "Though having Luke would be a bonus. Where is he right now, overseas, doing what?"

Ryan shrugged. Luke's team was called up and shipped out sometimes with no notice at all. His schedule had become more and more of a mystery, especially of late.

Marcus reached for a vest and tossed another to Ryan. "Put it on," he said, pulling his over his t-shirt, feeling the chill in the air. The mosquitoes were out, and he slapped the back of his neck when he felt a bite. "Leave the phones in the trunk, and yeah, take out the SIM and battery."

He reached for two flashlights and opened the gun case to pull out a Ruger. In the back of the trunk was the Faraday bag Luke had given him one day not long ago, a few months back, he thought.

He held the Ruger out to Ryan and said, "Take it," then pulled the SIM and battery out of his phone and tossed it all in the bag. He waited as Ryan checked the safety on the gun and the ammo clip, then took the holster Marcus held out.

"I get we're going in blind without a radio, but someone needs to know where we are," Ryan said. "So do we give good old Dad a call?"

The helicopter was louder, and Marcus knew it would be only moments before it was right above them. He closed the trunk and stepped away from the car into the trees with Ryan just as the lights shone past them. Damn, they needed to hide it better. As the helicopter moved away, Marcus wondered how much time they had.

They were being circled, which meant Rafe was being circled. How long before he ran again? Marcus knew Raymond O'Connell, a.k.a. Jake, was about as covert as they came.

"You mean so he can do what he does best, stay under the radar and fill in Harold without anyone knowing what we're doing, then figure out a way to get the spotlight off where we are?" Marcus held out his hand. "Give me your phone. I'll call."

As Marcus dialed his mom's cell phone, knowing his dad would likely answer, Ryan headed back to the trunk to grab some water and a backpack, as well as spare ammo, the first aid kit, and anything else he thought they needed.

"Where are you?" Raymond said. The phone hadn't even rung. Like, how did he do that?

"Oh, up shit creek, basically about half a click off where they're looking. We won't have our cell phones, and we're going to be on foot. Harold is back at the station. Let him know a roadblock was set up where I radioed Therese that we lost one of the prisoners. Tell him they have Tracy. He'll fill you in. Ryan and I are hiking in the back way. Harold knows where we're going, but my conversation on the radio was recorded. Not sure what the fuck is going on, but someone wants both these guys dead, and one is already."

His dad was quiet at first. "Use that Faraday bag Luke gave you," he finally said, "and hide your car. You check in two hours from now. Don't call the station. Call this cell. You need anything?"

"Nope, just some luck. Oh, yeah, and have Harold find out where they took Tracy. Told her to lawyer up and shut the fuck up."

"I'll tell him," Raymond said. "Watch your back, and watch your brother's."

Then his dad hung up, and Marcus wondered if he'd ever settle things with Raymond O'Connell.

"Well?" was all Ryan said. He held open the Faraday bag, and Marcus removed the SIM and battery from Ryan's phone and tossed them in. Ryan then sealed it and tossed it in the backpack before looping it over his shoulder.

"We need to hide the car," Marcus said. "Two-hour check-in. Let's go."

He closed the trunk, and Ryan handed him the keys. Marcus climbed in the car and pulled ahead, closer to the bush, as close as he could get without getting stuck. He heard the scrape of branches and knew he was scratching it up good. He turned off the car and stepped out, shoving the keys in his pocket. Ryan was dragging two heavy fir branches over to cover the car. Together, they added three more, then tossed on a few smaller ones, just enough that it wouldn't be visible from the air.

"Good enough. How far do you think?" Marcus wiped his hands together and took the flashlight Ryan handed him.

"Not far, probably thirty minutes, if that, to where the pile of lumber is. From there, what did Tracy say? He could be anywhere. There are a lot of places to hide. I can get you there, but from there, it's up to you. Shouldn't have to point this out to you, because I know you know this, but he's already seen his friend gunned down, and he doesn't know you aren't going to do the same. Does he have weapons? Military training? His girlfriend isn't with us anymore to talk him down, so how're you going to handle this, brother? A man who's got nothing to lose isn't going to ask questions first. You and I are basically collateral." Ryan shone his flashlight to a nearby bush, where Marcus could just make out a trail.

"Just get me there," he said. "I'll figure it out. If anything, I'm good at talking my way out of things and convincing most to see reason."

His brother made a rude noise under his breath. "Not always, Marcus, and this time, you have both sides against you."

Ryan started walking, and Marcus fell in behind, brushing back the branches of an overgrown trail, bush-whacking. There was one thing his brother hadn't mentioned: their family. He could always count on his brothers, his sisters, his mom, and Raymond O'Connell.

"You may be right, Ryan, but you forgot something important."

His brother shone his flashlight back to him and stopped. "And what is that?"

"You, good old Dad, Owen, Luke, Karen, Suzanne, and Mom. We always have each other's backs. So I disagree, because there's always a third side. Our side."

Ryan said nothing, just flicked his flashlight around and started walking again. "Fine, I stand corrected. Just let me know how we're going to play this."

Marcus could hear the chopper in the distance along with barking dogs, too. "I think we're going to have to play it by ear. Just get me there. The only thing we can count on is to expect the unexpected."

CHAPTER 10

The tarp-covered wood was exactly as Tracy had described, stacked about six by five feet, from one glance. Marcus stopped with Ryan, shining his light over the rocks holding the tarp down, which appeared undisturbed, and then over to what looked like a flat enough place to build a cabin. Amid the trees, the night was quiet aside from the helicopter he thought he could still hear in the distance. The dogs not so much anymore. The silence bothered him in ways he couldn't quite put into words as he glanced at his watch. It was now three thirty in the morning, and time was not on their side.

"Tick-tock, Marcus," Ryan said in a low voice from behind him, having flicked his flashlight off.

Marcus let his shine just past the flat spot over something that seemed out of place, white metal. "Think that's the truck over there?"

Ryan flicked his flashlight back on and walked to the

other side of the tarped-over lumber, and Marcus followed. "You want to check it out?"

The last thing he wanted to do, feeling the hair stand on the back of his neck and up his back, was walk out into the open anywhere. He knew that feeling, as if someone were watching him.

"Ryan, shut it off," he said, gesturing to the flashlight. He didn't have to say any more to his brother, knowing he'd move back out of the way and behind him. They'd done too much together, growing up, the kinds of things that skirted the law, and had saved each other's asses more times than he could count. They really did know each other well.

"Rafe Jackson!" Marcus called out. "Tracy Mitchell told me where to find you. I'm Sheriff Marcus O'Connell, from Livingston. I know what happened to Holter. I was at the scene and know it was staged. I need you to come out so I can talk to you." He paused, because calling out too loudly was risky. He didn't know who else was around. "Rafe, I don't know how close they are, but there's a shoot to kill order out on you. The only way to end this is for you to come out and let me take you in alive so you can stay that way."

He stopped talking, sure he'd heard a branch, some rustling.

Ryan tapped his shoulder. "Marcus, over there," he whispered, and he flashed his light over to where a bush swayed.

Marcus pulled his SIG and moved through the bushes, listening to branches crack underfoot as he hurried in the only direction he could go, moving on instinct. Someone stumbled ahead, he thought. Ryan was right behind him as he ran, and then his light flicked over someone.

"Stop!" Marcus shouted. "I'm not going to kill you, but if you keep running, I'll shoot, and then everyone will hear."

The man, who wore the same dirty brown prison pants and shirt as Donnelly had, got to his feet and started running again. Marcus hurried, knowing he was fast, branches slapping at him. He hoped to hell he wouldn't trip. He couldn't see the uneven ground.

Then the man went down in front of him again, and his light shone at a bank that dropped right off. He heard a scuffle, a skid, a thump over dirt and branches, the unmistakable sound of someone falling down a hill.

Marcus slipped on his ass as he went down the steep bank, his light on the prisoner, who rolled and slid and then stumbled, hitting a tree. He was almost there. He skidded and slipped and ran, lifting his gun, which he'd almost lost, along with the flashlight, shining it on the man. He flicked off the safety with an audible click in the silence of the night. He was right on him, making his way over, doing his damnedest to keep his footing.

"Don't get up, Rafe," he yelled. "I do not want to shoot you, but I will if you keep running. Stay down."

Rafe held a hand up over his face against the light. Another step closer, and Marcus felt he might bolt or do something.

"Stay down, Rafe Jackson! Don't do it. I told you Tracy sent me. If you move, I'll shoot, and gunfire can be heard a long way. The only thing standing between you and a slab in the morgue is me." He was sweating. Ryan was behind him, but Rafe was looking for a way out, which made him dangerous.

The man moved so damn fast around the tree, debris rustling as he skidded further down the hill with an *oomph*. Marcus flicked his safety back on and holstered his gun, holding his flashlight up as he slid on his ass again.

Rafe was sliding fast down the hill, but Ryan had reached him. Marcus rolled, a rock jabbing in his leg, his side. He stumbled and landed right beside them, and he was back on his feet, his gun out and the safety off, pressing it right to Rafe's head where he hovered over Ryan. It looked like he had landed a good punch, from the blood dripping from Ryan's lip.

"Get off my brother," Marcus said. "Hands up! I will pull the trigger."

Rafe slowly lifted his hands, and Marcus yanked his cuffs from his back pocket and slapped one on. Ryan slid out and stood, and Marcus holstered his gun and pushed Rafe on the ground, pulling his arm behind his back and cuffing both wrists. He pulled him up and over.

"Sit down there," he said. "You okay, Ryan?"

Ryan was breathing hard. "Fine, you?"

Marcus rested his hands on his belt and shone the light on Rafe again. "Never fucking better," he said. He heard the dogs again in the distance. The chopper, he figured, was at least ten clicks away, too. "We need to get the hell out of here. You hear those dogs, Rafe? The closer they get, the less I'm able to save your ass."

"And why the fuck would you give a shit about me?

What the fuck have you done with Tracy?" His hair was a mess, debris in it.

Marcus reached down, grabbed his arm, and held it. "Get up. Walk," he said, knowing he sounded pissed. He flicked his flashlight up the hill he'd slid most of the way down. "Ryan, which way? Tell me there's an easier way up."

His brother said nothing. Rafe wasn't done fighting back either, he thought. It was a sense he got from dealing with the many people he'd arrested. There were those who were compliant and those who'd stop at nothing to get away.

"What the hell did you do with Tracy?" Rafe said again. "Leave her alone. She's got nothing to do with this."

"Over here, Marcus." Ryan shone the flashlight at him, showing him the path.

"Move," Marcus said, his grip firm on Rafe. The man was his height, the kind of lean that might fool someone into thinking he wasn't strong. But he was wily.

They started walking the edge of the narrow path. The part up ahead was steep, and Ryan was waiting there.

"Tracy was with us," Marcus said, "but a roadblock was set up where I lost you before. They were listening on the radio, heard everything, and they know about her. I couldn't stop them from taking her. I told her to ask for a lawyer, say nothing, which is why I need to get you back to Livingston, out of here. They really want you bad, Rafe. Sure, I get the prison break thing, but what I don't get is that it seems someone wants you dead. I have a ton of questions, and no one is answering. Did Holter really give himself up?"

Rafe pulled his arm, which had Marcus really digging in. He knew the man would be bruised, for sure. "He knew I was struggling, but I'd have carried him into hell," Rafe said. "He told me to go. I was tired, and we'd gone miles. He'd buggered his leg, his ankle, and couldn't put anything on it. We moved as fast as we could, him hopping, me carrying as much of his weight as I could, but they were still gaining on us. I kept saying no, but he just pulled away and yelled. I couldn't believe he did that. I'm still sick over it. How could he do that to us, to me?

"He didn't look back. I knew my only choice was to run, the only way I was going to be able to save him. I'd made it over the hill when I heard the shot. I made my way back, and what I saw was worse than anything I'd seen in the military. He was cuffed, his hands behind his back, face down, blood pouring out of his back, unmoving. I knew he was dead, and there were four or five of them, dogs too, standing around. Murderers, all of them."

He heard dogs again in the distance and was sure they were coming that way. He was behind Rafe, urging him, knowing he'd just have to fall back and it would take Marcus with him. "You didn't see them shoot him," he said.

Rafe let out a rude sound. "Nope, but how dangerous is a man, a preacher, cuffed with his hands behind his back?"

Marcus didn't know what to say or how to even

begin to make sense of it, considering he'd be coming out against a lot of cops, prison guards, and Romi using the word of a criminal, an escaped convict. Yeah, he already knew it was political suicide.

"I don't know what to tell you," Marcus said, "but right now, the focus is getting you out of here. You hear them coming?"

Ryan was at the top of the hill, shining the light down. He reached for Rafe's other arm and pulled him up over the last steep part while Marcus put his hand down on the bank and pulled himself up behind him.

"We need to pick up the pace," Ryan said. "Any thoughts on what to do? Do we go right to the station or what? They could be waiting for you as soon as we drive back."

Marcus had already thought of that. He wondered who else had been called in.

"Is check-in time coming up?" Ryan asked.

Marcus glanced at his watch. "Another forty minutes. As soon as we turn on a cell phone, if they have eyes on us, they have us." He reached for Rafe's arm and fell in behind Ryan. The path was easier now, and he realized they'd run farther than he thought.

"You send me back, I'm dead, you know," Rafe said.

Marcus shook his head. "How did you get out? You had to have help from inside. With the kind of security they have, no one walks out. Maybe explain to me who it is who wants you dead, a preacher and a vet from the streets. I'm blind here and seem to be out of the loop, so how about filling me in?"

"Marcus, pick up the pace," Ryan called back to him.

"Come on, pick it up." Marcus nudged Rafe, gripping his arm, wondering how far he'd run on foot. Damn, a long ways. He had to be tired.

Then Rafe's legs gave out, and he went down.

"Ryan, give me some water back here," Marcus called out, leaning down.

The adrenaline had left him. Nothing was left. He was drained, done. Marcus heard the zip of the backpack, and Ryan handed him a bottle of water. He tucked the flashlight in his belt and unscrewed the cap, squatting down and holding it to Rafe's lips.

"Come on, drink some," he said. He lifted it, and Rafe swallowed greedily, downing half the bottle before Marcus pulled it back. Water dripped down his face. "That's good for now," he said. "You good to walk?"

Rafe was breathing heavy. He nodded. "Yeah."

Marcus stood and handed the bottle back to Ryan, then reached down for Rafe's arm and helped him up. The man nodded and took a step. Marcus knew his brother was leading them out, trying to get them to hurry. The chopper was coming again, and Ryan was gesturing for them to move.

"There was no reason for us to be arrested," Rafe said, "but I saw it coming. Holter, he didn't back down from authority. He would call out tyranny, call out anyone he saw as deliberately hurting others. He said he could see evil in a man, no soul. I always thought he was just being weird, but when you're on the streets, trying to help the fallen, you realize something many don't. Those on the streets are there because of the evil in this world. You ever ask yourself about all the taxes you pay, federal, state, sales, property? Sit down and add it up. There are roughly 240 million people in this country. If you take just half of that and multiply it by what you pay, you come up with trillions. So where is the money?"

The path narrowed. Ryan disappeared through some bushes, and Marcus reached for his flashlight from his belt and flicked it on. "Okay, so I pay a lot," he said, thinking of his salary. "Never stopped to think of that. But we have roads and services..."

"You know when income tax came about?" Rafe said. Why the hell were they talking about taxes?

"I don't."

"To pay for the war. It was supposed to be temporary, and then it wasn't. Every year, taxes went up, more taxes added on to everything. The liberals want services, programs, but no one stops to say hey, wait a second, why and where and how? We need programs for vets who are fucked over because of wars these politicians keep creating. We need programs for the poor who are trying to make it, for the homeless, for addicts who are hooked on big pharma drugs and have lost everything. We need shelters, food stamps, welfare, charities for kids. I could go on. Look at every state agency and ask yourself why it exists.

"You know what Holter did? He knew there was supposed to be funding to help those on the streets, so he was on the doorsteps of city council members, aldermen, business owners. Then the cops would be out every time he rattled a cage, calling people out, trying to expose fraud. One shelter received hundreds of thousands of private donations from citizens and food from grocery stores paid for by bleeding hearts who had felt generous a time or two and given a few dollars. Yet when Holter managed to get a hold of their financials, you know what he found? Nearly all the money went toward paying the administrator's ridiculously high salary. Virtually nothing went to the people who needed the help. That's what he was fighting. The cops who came out to shut him down, shut him up, threaten him, ticket him, were all following orders from their captain. Some enjoyed what they had to do more than others."

"So you're saying Holter was arrested because of his activism? I have a hard time believing that. He was booked for uttering threats."

"Oh, he didn't threaten," Rafe said. "He promised. He meant every word he said. This one cop by the name of Ben Hughes seemed to really enjoy showing Holter and anyone else on the street that they had no voice. Holter told him to his face that he would personally see him to hell. He wouldn't give him directions; he'd walk him right in there. No matter what he tried to do, Holter wouldn't back down. The first time Ben hit him, he got right back up. When he hit him again, even the old guy on the street told Holter to stay down, but he wouldn't.

"I was around the corner and came running when he got up again, and this time he hit that cop back. I knew what he'd done. I yelled and ran in there only to have a gun in my face. We found ourselves both cuffed, sirens blasting. Hughes had already called for backup, and the story was our word against not only that of a cop but also a business man who just happened to be walking by, the owner of an electronics store who hated all the homeless around there, and two other cops who had shown up and repeated Hughes's story."

Marcus spotted the clearing just ahead. Ryan put up a hand to stop, flicking off his flashlight, and so did Marcus, moving closer under a fir tree. The helicopter was right above them, shining a light over the tarped-over lumber in the small clearing. Marcus said nothing.

Rafe was still beside him, his hands cuffed behind him. For the first time in Marcus's life, he felt as if he were the one being hunted.

The helicopter moved past them, and the ground thundered and vibrated from its power as it retreated.

"Why are you doing this?" Rafe said to him.

Marcus flicked on his flashlight, and Ryan did too, gesturing for them to move. "Because it's my job," he said.

Rafe stumbled a bit, and Marcus gripped his arm harder, knowing he'd likely have marks, as well. "Seriously?"

"Yeah, my job, which I love, and the fact that I swore an oath to the Constitution to protect the people of this county, one of whom is now you. You know, some of us really do believe in right and wrong and the truth getting out. So as soon as we get back to the station, you're going to tell me everything. I believe you're right about one thing: Dead men can't talk, and someone doesn't want you talking. Maybe you should start with who helped you break out of prison."

CHAPTER 11

"You can't come back here," Raymond said. The phone had rung only once before he answered.

A chorus of birds was chirping at the approaching dawn even though it was still dark out, and something about the energy of night had Marcus wondering what the hell was going on. He rested his hand against a tree. Ryan was pulling branches from the car, and the back door was open, Rafe tucked inside.

"Why?" Marcus said. "What's going on?"

He heard voices, then a door closing, then quiet. His dad's voice had been low, a warning, so of course, Marcus had a ton of questions.

"Pretty sure you already know," Raymond said. "Feds are here. They've basically taken over your office, put a tap on the phone line, and questioned Harold, Therese, and Colby. Harold is back in there again behind closed doors, and I've been asked to leave. No civilians."

"And they didn't ask who you were?"

"Sure, they asked. Colby offered up that I'm your mom's boyfriend. He was more than helpful to them, if you understand what I'm saying. Therese wondered, I know. She sees too much, more than you think. The feds have asked where you are, and the phones are ringing off the hook from residents, the prison warden, two different sheriffs from neighboring counties, the state troopers office, basically anyone and everyone. They know Ryan is with you. They've got a tracker on your phone and your car, and they know you went dark. Five seconds now, and you hang up and pull that battery and SIM back out. You remember where Luke used to go to hide out for days on end, how far he hiked? No one found him. You understand what I'm saying?"

Strong, clipped, to the point. Had his dad always been this way?

"Ah, fuck," Marcus said. "So they're coming. How long do we have?"

"Less time than you need. You're resourceful, smart, a problem solver. Time's up. Go," was all his dad said before hanging up.

Marcus squeezed his cell phone, then pulled out the battery and SIM card, shaking his head. He reached for the Faraday bag in the backpack and shoved everything back in, then headed over to Ryan, his flashlight shining on the ground. Ryan pulled the last of the big branches off, and Marcus reached for the hunting knife he always carried, holstered on his belt. He pulled it out and stabbed the back tire, hearing the air whoosh.

"Marcus, what the fuck?" Ryan snapped.

Marcus pulled the knife back out, and the back end

dropped from the flattened tire. "We're on foot now," he said. "Shit has hit the fan, and I'm not sure who's coming, but whoever it is and however many, they won't be long. Remember where Luke's hideaway is?"

He tucked the knife back in its leather holster on his belt and pulled his keys from his pocket to open the trunk and grab half a dozen more bottles of water. He tucked them in the backpack along with a box of granola bars Charlotte had bought for him, telling him to carry them just in case. Damn, he really loved her.

He tossed in more cartridges for his assault rifle, then zipped up the backpack and slammed the trunk. Ryan appeared beside him, wide eyed, as he opened the driver's door, and the inside light popped on.

"What's going on?" he said. "Yeah, I know where that is. I'm guessing ten clicks or so, maybe more, not an easy walk, and up some steep terrain."

Marcus tossed Ryan the heavy backpack and reached in between the seats to pull out the assault rifle. They were still in their vests. He closed the door. "We need to move, because they'll be tracking this car, and I guarantee you we don't have much time."

"Dad told you that?"

Marcus gave Ryan a look. His brother was angry—at him? No. At a situation that was snowballing faster than he could ever have imagined.

"So, what, we're going to hike up to a hideout made by a kid and do what, Marcus? This is fucking insane," Ryan said, and Marcus didn't miss the frustration in his brother's voice, because it was exactly what he was feeling. "You didn't tell me what he said."

Marcus knew who the "he" was: good old Dad. "Convergence on my office. Feds and everyone took it over and have been interrogating Harold, Colby, and Therese. They want Rafe, but I'm starting to get the feeling they want me tucked safely away someplace and my hands tied so I can't do nothing. It seems as if suddenly, we're being hunted because I'm the loose thread here. They find us, they take Rafe Jackson. I may not have been sure before, but I am now: If they do, he won't be alive long enough to see the light of day, let alone make it back to prison. I'm not so sure him talking to me is enough anymore. Even recording whatever it is he knows, I don't think I could do anything with it."

Marcus walked around the car to the open back door and tucked his flashlight into his belt after flicking it off. "Change of plans, Rafe," he said, reaching for his arm. The man's hands were still cuffed behind him. Of course, he had to be uncomfortable.

"What's going on?" Rafe said. "You said you were taking me back to Livingston."

"Well, I also said I'm keeping you alive, and right now, we can't go back. The people looking for you have taken over my office. Come on. They'll be on their way here, so we have to move."

He helped him out, then gave the door a shove closed, holding his rifle in one hand. He walked around to where Ryan waited, flashlight on, and just took in the terrain. He didn't have a clue which way to go.

"This way," Ryan said and started walking across the narrow trail, crossing the opposite way, down an embankment. Marcus followed with Rafe.

"Would be easier if you uncuffed me," Rafe said as Marcus tapped his back, moving him ahead.

"It would be easier," Marcus said. "But the thing is, Rafe, the cuffs aren't coming off. Got a long walk. Get moving."

Ryan glanced back to them with his flashlight. It was eerily quiet, only their footsteps and the rustle of branches as a hint of light emerged on the distant horizon. Marcus knew he should've been tired, but he was running on pure adrenaline.

Rafe said nothing, just followed Ryan, who had shut off his flashlight the second the sunlight hit the sky. Marcus was very aware he'd not heard the dogs for some time now, but that didn't make him feel any better. He could hear water and knew a creek was just up ahead.

"We need to pick up the pace," he said in a low voice.

Ryan had pushed through the brush toward the creek, which was higher than usual, moving faster. He walked right down to the creek bed, scooped water in his hands and splashed his face, and then scooped more and drank it. The side of his mouth was swelling from where Rafe had hit him, but the blood had dried, and his blue eyes looked so damn frustrated and tired. Then Marcus heard it again, barking in the distance.

"We'll wade upriver about half a mile," Ryan said. "The dogs will lose the scent. Marcus, he can't have his hands behind his back in this. Too hard to balance as it is."

Marcus put his rifle down against a rock and pulled the key to the cuffs from his pocket. "Turn around," was all he said to Rafe. He unlocked one cuff on his left hand, then shoved the key back in his pocket and snapped the loose cuff on his own wrist. Lifting his hand, he took in the man. His brown eyes said nothing, but Marcus knew he was thinking. Ryan only shook his head.

Marcus leaned down and reached for the rifle, saying, "Let's go."

He wandered down to the water with Rafe, who scooped water over his face and hair with his free hand, then scooped some up to drink. Marcus gave him a second, then started walking, falling in behind Ryan, who moved through the water, up past his knees. The rocks were slick in places as they kept moving, the barking following them.

"You wanted to know who helped us get out," Rafe said.

For a second, Marcus didn't understand what he was saying. Then he did. "A guard?" he asked as they made it around a bend, trudging through the water, following his brother's steps.

"No one has any idea what they're in for when they become a prisoner. Even though the corrections staff work there day in and day out, you have no idea who all the staff are, what they believe, if they're good or bad. I never lost count of the days behind bars. As bad as conditions were for me, Holter had a target on him from the minute we stepped inside. He was forced into solitary confinement, strip searched, and humiliated. They would move him and keep him separated, away from me, because they knew I watched his back.

"Holter went to a part of the prison once reserved for murderers, the worst of the worst. They found ways to make sure he was somewhere I wasn't. Cons inside knew what was happening. Staff would try to get inmates to beat him up. Every time a prisoner is assaulted or murdered inside, someone on staff is behind it, and someone on the outside is behind them. You'll have to start with the bank accounts of the staffers and look into any one-time large deposits. From there you'll start to figure it out as the dots connect."

Ryan moved to the other side of the creek and pulled at a large branch to scamper up the edge. Rafe followed, basically pulling Marcus with him. The pinch of the cuffs kept him alert. He could still hear the dogs, but they'd be confused once they hit the water. Had they gone far enough upstream?

"If they get closer, you're going to want to let me go," Rafe said. "You think you'll stay alive if they catch you with me? You and your brother are collateral. They'll tell a convincing story, and it will be pinned on me. I'll be dead too, so no one will question it."

"No one is letting anyone go," Marcus said. "You still didn't tell me who helped you escape. You have any proof that the prison staff were paid off, and which ones?"

Rafe was keeping up with Ryan, who was just ahead of them, moving at a pace that was pushing Marcus harder than he had been pushed in a long time. The trail started to climb, narrow, steep in places, and the brush was thick.

"Oh, I know which ones—or have an idea," Rafe said. "But proof? Nothing I have access to. The judge who sentenced us imposed a publication ban, and when Holter brought up the missing money from the non-profit shelter he'd been fighting with, saying it was the reason he was targeted, it was stricken from the record. That fucking public defender was as useless as a tit on a bull. I told Holter to knock it off. When you have the weight of their side coming at you, you understand really fucking quickly that they own the DA, the judge, the courts, the jails, and the system.

"Even inside prison, though, Holter wouldn't stop. They knew he wouldn't until they saw whatever beaten-down expression they wanted to see. I swear the guards there know exactly how to bring a man to his knees. Physical and psychological torture will break most men, but I think they underestimated Holter's strength and will. He's made no secret of his life's purpose and who he works for: God.

"He said he was a voice for women and orphans, for the poor, and he would always come out against the ridiculous programs they wanted to toss money at. You know which 'they' we're talking about, the city, the county, the state, the country. The number of programs would blow the average person's mind," Rafe said, then slipped and went down on his knees, nearly taking Marcus with him.

Ryan glanced back from way up the trail and called out, "You two okay?"

"Yeah," was all Marcus said, still gripping his rifle, taking in how tired Rafe looked. "You want water?"

Rafe rolled on his knees, shaking his head. Marcus could still hear dogs, but he thought they were farther away. He knew Rafe had to hear them too, as he got back on his feet and reached for a branch to pull himself up the steep trail. Marcus struggled, hampered by his one hand cuffed and his other gripping the rifle. He looked back at how far they'd come.

"How much farther?" he said, though he had a vague idea.

Ryan let his gaze settle on Rafe and then Marcus. "Not much, but we need to pick it up," he said. Then he started walking. Rafe fell in behind him with Marcus.

"Jail isn't supposed to be pleasant, but you're saying Holter was targeted inside?" Marcus said. He didn't know what to think. He knew the inner politics of jails didn't differ much from those of criminal gangs on the streets.

"Holter believed standing in his truth was the only way," Rafe said. "He said as much, told me to be brave. Damn near knocked him in the teeth for that. The problem is that Holter took on the system out there, the politicians. When they came up with this plan to end homelessness, he was in their faces, saying they would never get rid of the homeless problem because there's no help for the poor who end up on the streets. Add in mental illness, and some people can't be in a shelter, can't function. The places that offered help to them were shut down decades ago.

"I met Holter when I went looking for a man from my unit, Levy. He'd fallen off the radar. The war over there left him fucked up, so much so that he couldn't reintegrate back here. It was hard for all of us, and there was no help. Holter knew everyone out there and their reasons for being on the street, or at least he had an idea. He never turned his back on Levy. Me and the guys in my unit, we got him off the street, cleaned up, and pooled enough money to get him the kind of help that was never going to come from any government or the system that did this to him, to us.

"I knew what Holter was up against. Any other sane person would have walked away, because he really was in the middle of a David and Goliath fight, but he wasn't scared. In fact, that was what drove him. I'd never seen that kind of strength or sense of right and wrong in anyone. While we were locked up, he'd tell the guards that he'd pray for them, that he forgave them. I watched as one punched him in the face and then beat him with his stick, then leaned down and said, 'Pray for that.'

"It didn't end there. It was a series of psychological torture. For everything that happened to me for trying to defend him in there, it was ten times worse for him. I spent weeks on end locked in a metal box, stripped naked, one time for fifty-eight days straight. The guards would appear after what seemed like days but was likely only hours, and the door would open. A nurse would take my pulse and vitals, offer me drugs—antidepressants, Vicodin, opiates, a big pharma candy store. I told them to fuck off. The door would slam shut. Repeat over and over. You have any idea the number of inmates who just take the drugs and get hooked?"

They were winding their way up the trail, and Rafe stopped talking.

"How much farther, Ryan?" Marcus said. He was trying to remember how long it had been since he'd been up there. Years. He listened, and he couldn't hear the dogs anymore. He'd heard nothing of a chopper, either, and the sun was making its way up in the sky.

"Over that ridge," was all Ryan said as he put one foot in front of the other, carrying the backpack full of supplies that would hold them for a bit.

"You think the shelter Luke built is still there?"

Ryan said nothing at first, just glanced back as he stepped around a tree on the path, then pushed another big fir branch out of the way. Marcus could tell by his expression that he'd heard everything Rafe said. "We'll see what's still standing when we get there."

Rafe stopped, out of breath, and leaned down, his hands on his knees.

"We don't have much farther," Marcus said.

Rafe only nodded and kept walking, pulling at the cuff. Marcus gripped his rifle, feeling the sweat beading down his back, under his arms. He needed a shower, a bed, his wife, but that wasn't happening anytime soon.

"I know you don't believe me," Rafe said, and Marcus didn't know how to reply.

"You still haven't told me who got you out, you and Holter," he said, "and the reason for this manhunt, shooting Holter down. Someone doesn't want you talking, and I have to wonder, what is it they don't want you talking about?"

Rafe stopped and faced him. "You know how I doubled back after I heard the shot and saw them standing over Holter's body?"

Marcus didn't say anything, just waited.

"Three guards from the prison were there. One of them, his name is Steven Hardwell. He was the one who got us out, but he was standing over Holter with the other two. I knew it was too easy how he moved us to a storage room in the prison, then out a side door, a back entrance, an unmanned, unlocked door. He slipped us into his trunk and dropped us a mile away, where we ran. And we kept running. He just happened to be with the guards hunting us down, the dogs, and the cops who shot Holter. Do I know which one pulled the trigger?" Rafe shrugged and made an expression of disillusionment or anger. The way he talked, Marcus figured he was good at compartmentalizing everything. "You think just maybe they were told to shoot us? What better way to get rid of us than to help us break out and then hunt us down? There are still questions asked in prison. If one of us were killed, okay, but both? Tracy was making a lot of noise, doing what she could. But if we broke out, think about the story. They would control the narrative."

Then Rafe turned away and started walking again, and Marcus fell in behind, knowing that if what he'd said was true, something sinister was going on.

CHAPTER 12

"Hey, what the hell?" Ryan said, then laughed, Marcus thought, as he walked with Rafe, pushing through the bushes. Ahead, his brother Luke walked right over to Ryan and gave him a hug, then a slap on the back and a wide smile. Luke's hair was shorter again, wavy brown, and he let his gaze fall on Marcus and then Rafe through his sunglasses.

"You look like absolute shit there, Marcus," he said. "A little out of shape?"

Damn, he hadn't expected this. Something about Luke being there warmed Marcus in ways he didn't think he could have put into words. "Didn't know you were back," he said.

Luke said nothing as he approached the shelter, which appeared more like a bushcraft A-frame than a lean-to. Marcus wondered if it had been shored up over the years.

Ryan dumped the backpack in front of it and pushed

back a tarp that covered what looked like a door. "Did you fix this up?" he called out.

Luke reached for the rifle Marcus was carrying. "Just added a few things, made it dry to hold up to the weather," he said without turning around, running a safety check on the rifle, checking the slide, looking down the chamber, unloading and loading the rounds. It was just second nature and something Marcus always saw his brother doing.

Luke glanced over his shoulder to Ryan and then back to Marcus, nodding to the cuff on his wrist. "Necessary?" was all he asked.

Marcus knew what he meant, and he reached into his pocket and pulled out the key. "Yeah," he said. "Is there a spot I can cuff him?"

Luke gestured behind him. "Take your pick of trees, or try that chair I made over there. Should be enough to hold him."

Marcus took in a chair made from large branches sawed down and fastened with rope, by the looks of it. His brother had always been resourceful. He unfastened the cuff from his wrist and walked Rafe over to the chair, which was shaped like an Adirondack, outside the shelter, under the heavy brush.

"Sit down," he said and clipped the cuff to one of the thick round branches used to make the chair. He gave a yank, seeing that it was secure, then stepped back just as Ryan came out of the shelter. Ryan tossed him a bottle of water, then handed one down to Rafe, who unscrewed the cap and took a long swallow.

"Your timing is impeccable," Marcus said to Luke,

who let his gaze linger long and hard on Rafe before looking back to him.

"Just have this sixth sense, you know, for when you manage to get yourself in over your head. You really stepped into it this time, Marcus, I have to say. So what's the plan?"

Ryan said nothing, just handed Rafe a granola bar.

"No idea," Marcus said. "Kind of making it up as I go."

He couldn't see Luke's eyes behind his sports sunglasses, likely from his job. He was in camo pants and a matching long-sleeved shirt. His brother could blend in and go to ground better than all of them.

"And how's that working out for you?" Luke said. Marcus wondered at times if Luke enjoyed rubbing it in.

"Well, I'm sure you're dying to tell me, so fill me in," Marcus said. "Guess good old Pops sent you up here. Sounds like the manhunt is underway, and if they find him, he's dead. Don't understand the reason they're so intent. He's given me a bunch of bullshit and stuff, but I can tell you his friend Holter was shot in the back. Rafe said he turned himself in, was injured, slowing them down. He gave himself up so Rafe could get away. Rafe doubled back after he heard the shot. The scene had been staged by the time I arrived with Suzanne. The only thing they wanted was for me to sign off and get the fuck out of there. Seems these two really stepped on the wrong toes."

"Or it's gone too far, and the only way to end this is for him to be six feet under," Luke said. "Less questions that way. Haven't even been home yet, but Dad filled me in. One thing he knows is an exit strategy. He's mastered that. So here I am. Your stationhouse has been taken over. Think Pops was reaching out to Jack. In the meantime, Marcus, what is your plan here? Because the way I see it, they want him, and you ain't going to be able to walk out of here with him or take him to Livingston and put him safely back in jail. What's the desired outcome?"

He knew what his brother was doing. Marcus also knew Luke would have his back, whatever he needed. "The outcome is everyone staying alive."

Luke nodded and glanced down to Rafe, who was shoving the last of the granola bar in his mouth.

"Sheriff," Rafe said, "you and I both know the only outcome here is me in the morgue. How many are looking for me? Here we are, in the middle of nowhere, and you still have me cuffed so I can't go anywhere. I get you're trying to keep me alive long enough to get me back down, handed off, and back to jail. Let's say that by some miracle, we make it back and you keep me alive. You stick me in a cell for five minutes in Livingston, but the guard who helped me and Holter out will be waiting. Then there's the warden, who's going to demand to know who let us out, unless he already knows. That's a lot of somebodies who don't want anyone knowing their part in any of this. I can think of a dozen ways I'll die mysteriously before I ever make it back to prison. Told you to just let me go. Either I'm going to disappear, or they'll find me."

Marcus knew he was right, but he'd found himself in some pretty hairy situations before. "Not happening. I told you that already. You think I haven't had to figure out difficult shit before? I'll figure out something now." He hadn't meant for it to come out so sharply. No one said anything for a minute.

Ryan rested his arm against a heavy branch above his head, made a face, and looked over to him. "You know, Marcus, you've thought us out of some difficult spots, but this time, I can't see what your options are. I heard everything Rafe said to you about the toes he was stepping on. Even I have my eyes open enough to know that the programs funded endlessly by our tax dollars should have every one of the homeless living comfortably or getting the help they need, but it doesn't work that way. I asked Jenny a while ago, with all these programs, these non-profits, these shelters, where is the money going? Rafe, you said Holter was talking about that missing money."

Rafe took a swallow from his water bottle. "Holter had been digging for a long time into the missing money, not in just one area but the entire system. One shelter received close to a million in funding for beds, programs, miscellaneous shit, but in the end, there weren't enough beds, and most of the staff were volunteers. I knew the money was being funneled out the back door in high administrative salaries and other programs that didn't exist. He found it all.

"Cops were always being sent by the city about something someone made up. The day before the shit went down with that one cop, Holter met with one of the ward council members and showed his evidence that the money wasn't going where it was supposed to. He knew who was running the non-profit, and he had kept track of the grants coming from federal agencies, as well as state funds and private donations. He knew every community leader who had been involved at one time and presently. The ward councilor was named Nancy Taylor. She said she would dig into it. She dug into it, all right."

He gestured toward them with his water, and the cuff on his one wrist clinked as it pulled against Luke's chair. "I told Tracy some but not all," he said. "She was just trying to get us out, get me out. Now Tracy could have a target on her because of me. You understand what I'm saying?"

Ryan didn't look away from Rafe, and Luke was his same quiet self. He looked over at Marcus and motioned for him to step away with him so it was just them. Marcus took in the view, the trees, the mountains. Luke had picked this spot as a kid, and he'd never realized the beauty of it until now.

"You need an exit strategy here, Marcus," Luke said. "Not stepping on your toes, but I'm saying you've got a lot of people looking for this guy. There's still a shoot to kill order out on him. Now, I'm not saying I believe a word he says, but I've been in enough situations with bad guys who were supposed to be on my side to know that your enemy isn't always who you think it is."

Marcus wasn't sure what Luke was trying to say. "You're not telling me to let him go, are you?"

Luke made a face, looking out into the valley. "Wouldn't dream of doing that. This has to be your choice, Marcus. You're the one who has the badge and has to answer for all of this. Sometimes, Marcus, the right thing to do isn't what you think it is. All I'm saying is someone stepped on the wrong toes here. The man you've found isn't a cold-blooded killer who's going to rape women and children or kill them in their sleep."

Luke hadn't always been so cryptic, Marcus thought. "I think you know he isn't. He's a vet who was helping out a preacher on the streets. Tempers were lost."

Luke laughed roughly and shook his head, then handed Marcus his rifle. "Choice time, Marcus. I can stay up here for days and be comfortable."

"I just want justice here, Luke, and to do the right thing."

Luke said nothing. He lifted his sunglasses, and those blue eyes that carried so much landed hard on him, and he didn't look away. Evidently, he was done talking.

"How do I know if I've made the right choice?" Marcus said.

Luke pulled his arms over his chest. "When does any of us ever know?"

Damn, he didn't want to do this, but he could feel time ticking, and with that, a window was closing. He was damned either way, he thought. He glanced back to his brother and Rafe, who were talking, though about what, he had no idea. He gripped his rifle and then turned to his brother, knowing Luke would do whatever he asked. The loyalty ran river-deep.

He slapped a hand over his brother's shoulder. "If he's found…"

Luke shook his head. "He won't be," he said.

Marcus knew what his brother was saying. He only nodded, then started walking back over to Rafe, knowing

Ryan was tracking each step. He reached into his pocket and pulled out the key to the cuffs, then held out his rifle to Ryan, who took it for him.

Marcus stepped back and took in a man he barely knew. He leaned down, shoved the key in the cuff, and set him free, taking in the open question staring back at him.

"I don't understand," was all Rafe said. He didn't get up.

"I'll leave you some water," Marcus said. "Good luck to you."

Then he held out his hand. Rafe hesitated, wary, but stood up and took it. He said nothing as Marcus pulled away, gestured to Ryan, and said, "We're done here. Let's go home."

CHAPTER 13

Marcus lost his footing on a rock halfway across the creek and went down in the water, his head under. He damn near lost his rifle, grabbing it from the bed of the creek as he went over on his knees. He heard laughter from Ryan as he sat there, water running over his face, taking in the late afternoon sun. He'd been tired before, but it seemed for a moment as if everything had been sucked out of him. He just sat there in the water, his gun wet, his ammo, his duty belt, right down to his underwear.

"What, are you going to sit there all day?" Ryan said. "Suit yourself. Figure this is as good a place as any to fire up our cell phones." He dumped the backpack by a tree at the edge of the bank.

Marcus pushed himself up and waded the rest of the way over. Maybe Ryan knew how done he was, as he reached a hand out, and Marcus took it. His brother gave a hard yank, pulling him up the embankment, and Marcus set his rifle down against a tree.

"You know, for the last hour, I've wondered if I did the right thing," Marcus said. "He's still a criminal. He was charged by the court. I'm not a judge, but I sure as shit am supposed to uphold the law."

"Is he a criminal, Marcus?" Ryan said. "Be careful. There's a fuck-load of politics in your job, but right is still right."

For a moment, he didn't know what his brother was saying, and maybe the confusion knitting his brow was why Ryan let out a heavy, frustrated sigh. He pulled a bottle of water from the backpack and held it out to Marcus, who hesitated a second before taking it, unscrewing the cap, and drinking as Ryan pulled out a bottle for himself.

"Marcus, I'm not a sheriff, but I know enough from being a park warden to realize that sometimes we're given orders that come down from someplace, and we don't question them even though we know they're not right. You swore an oath to the Constitution, but I've been starting to wonder more and more as of late who the good guys really are. You ever wonder who's in jail? Like, really wonder? Jails are for dangerous criminals, murderers, rapists, but those types of convicts make up only maybe ten percent, and that's being generous.

"So who are the rest? Petty criminals who pissed off the wrong person. I've heard that eighty-five percent are the poor, in for drugs, theft, unpaid tickets, contempt, assaults, mischief. Think about it. If you have money and do the same crime, you'll never be arrested, let alone put in jail. A rich guy steals money from a bunch of pensioners, you know, millions, but no one can prove it, evidence disappears, or some politician steps in after getting a payday somewhere along the way.

"Many jails are private. They get a certain number of dollars per head, so the more people they shove in, the more money they make, and all of this is funded by you and me, the taxpayers. Then look at who owns the jails and the shelters. One thing Rafe said stuck with me: Shelters are also paid per head. Maybe one day I'll ask Jack how budgets really work, how money is allocated, and who gets to decide that taxing us to build our own prisons is a good idea.

"I mean, I think we all need to start looking at these so-called programs. And I'm not talking welfare. I'm talking government agencies and the programs within each one. I swear they're endless, and they aren't helping anyone. I'm starting to think Rafe was right about a lot of things. You think it was more that Holter was stirring things up, shining a spotlight where someone, or many someones didn't want one shone? If people are questioning money disappearing, that's never a good thing."

Marcus just stared at Ryan. He had downed half his bottle of water and felt pissed-off, on edge. The feeling just wouldn't go away, likely because his brother had just said out loud what Marcus suspected.

"You think Dad always knows where Luke is?" Marcus said.

Ryan shook his head, likely because he knew his brother didn't want to talk about the corruption that was right in their faces. "He knows something, that's for sure."

That was all Marcus was going to get. He knew he

was stalling because the questions that would be hammered at him were going to be grueling. The feds, the marshals, even Lester and the DA would all have something to ask him. Then there was Kellogg. Something about him wasn't sitting right in Marcus's mind.

"They're going to question you, Ryan," he said. "They'll ask the same questions over and over and try to trip you up. One thing very few people understand about cops is this mentality that's trained into them. Their first loyalty is to other cops, and they never trust citizens or the average person out there. Everyone is guilty until proven innocent, and most people are likely guilty of something, so just keep digging until you find it. Keep the pressure on until they crack. Most do." Marcus needed Ryan to understand. He sat on a stump and then downed the rest of his water.

"Guess that explains a lot of things," Ryan said. "But, again, I've got nothing to hide." He tossed his empty bottle in the backpack and pulled out the Faraday bag to retrieve his cell phone, SIM card, and battery, then tossed the bag over to Marcus. As soon as they powered their phones on, the hunters would know exactly where they were.

"You make sure you got your story straight, is all I'm saying," Marcus said, shoving the battery and SIM card in and powering up his phone at the same time as Ryan.

"What story?" Ryan said. "You and I searched all night on foot after your careless driving caused us to blow a tire. We've had no cell service. A mountain cat was hunting us, so we didn't make it to the highway. Call Harold to pick us up. Stop stalling."

Marcus glanced at his mailbox and messages, but he had no intention of listening to them, not right now. He pulled up the number to the stationhouse, then dialed Harold's cell instead.

"Where are you?" Harold snapped in a way he never had before.

"Ryan and I are likely about a mile from my cruiser. Blew a tire."

"Yeah, they know where your car is. You have any idea what the fuck is going on here?"

Marcus knew Ryan was watching him. His cell phone started ringing, and he answered.

"They find the prisoner, Jackson?" Marcus said.

There was silence. "No, but they sure as shit know you're fucking with them," Harold said. "You didn't find the missing prisoner?"

Marcus thought he heard voices. He shook his head. "Nope. Not a clue which way to look. We ran into a mountain cat that tracked us until sunrise, so we've just made it back this far. We couldn't get cell service until now. We need you to come and pick us up. We'll meet you at my car, if you can get a tow truck out for the tire."

He wasn't sure if Harold swore under his breath. He knew him well enough to know that he wasn't telling him everything. "Your car's already been towed. Just get back there. I'll pick you up."

Then he hung up at the same time Ryan did.

"Well, let's move," Marcus said. "Harold will pick us up. They already towed my car. Who called?" Marcus reached for the rifle, and Ryan slid the backpack over his shoulder.

"The director of Montana Fish and Game, wanting to know why I haven't answered," Ryan said. "Everyone is out looking for me, and I'm with you. You know, the usual questions I expected. Seems everyone is in on this." He started walking, and Marcus fell in behind.

"You going to have a problem there?" he said.

Ryan kept walking. "Only the same as you. Remember, we've been stuck out here all night, followed a trail, and had to deal with a mountain lion. And you can't drive worth shit."

Marcus heard the chopper again, and this time, as he looked up, feeling the pulse of it coming closer and then hovering above, he knew they had eyes on him and his brother. He lifted his hand in a wave at the chopper, and he wondered who else would be waiting for them along with Harold.

CHAPTER 14

Marcus was tired as all hell, and he needed a shower. He wasn't sure if it was anger at being toyed with that drove him, but his heart pounded as he walked through the front door of his station behind the two agents from the Marshals Service who had been waiting for him and Ryan where his cruiser had been. There hadn't been a sign of Harold or the car, and Marcus knew someone was up against him.

"We're going to need a formal statement from you, Sheriff," said the dark-haired agent. What was his name again? Garner.

Marcus rested a hand on the inner door of the station, gripping his rifle in the other, hearing the phones, voices, and general buzz of a crazed sheriff's office when a prisoner was on the loose. He took a second to glance back to the agents and Ryan, who was just behind them, beyond pissed.

"You want a statement from me?" Marcus said.

"Thanks for the ride, and watch yourself." He let his gaze linger, so done with these assholes.

He opened the inner door to find his wife behind her desk in her deputy shirt. Her beautiful hazel eyes reached out to him. She had been on the phone, but she hung up and hurried around the desk and into his arms, pressing a kiss to his lips. He pulled her close.

"Are you okay?" she said. "No one knew where you were. Harold said something about you and Ryan being out on foot all night…"

He didn't want to let her go. He kissed her again.

She wrinkled her nose. "You need a shower," she said.

He stepped back when he heard the door close behind him. Another agent, in dress pants, a white shirt, and a tie, with short light hair, was coming out of his office. "I need more than a shower," he said. "Who the fuck is that?"

Charlotte gave him a look that said she wasn't happy about it, either. "The feds, Sheriff Lester, and the Marshals Service. Everyone, it seems. They just came in and took over."

Harold was at his desk, his gaze guarded, and so was Therese. Marcus started walking to his office, taking in the agent with light hair standing at Colby's empty desk, dialing the phone as if he didn't give a shit who Marcus was.

"Well, well, Marcus O'Connell," Sheriff Lester called out from his office. "There you are. You fell right off the radar. Folks've been mighty worried about you. So where's the prisoner?"

Marcus just stood there, watching Lester sitting in his chair, behind his desk, appearing far too comfortable. He rested the rifle on Therese's desk. "I lost my balance in the water," he told her. "Went down in the creek bed, and so did this. I need you to take it apart and clean it so it doesn't rust. The shells are likely toast. Where's Colby?"

Ryan was talking with Charlotte, and Harold had said nothing, but Marcus knew something was wrong, off. Evidently, Harold's wings had been clipped, from the way he sat there, leaning back in his chair at an empty desk, his hands linked on his belt. The flicker of fire in his eyes told Marcus enough. A takeover of his office was well underway.

"He was sent home," Therese said. "Been here all night."

Marcus only glanced to his office again, where the old sheriff still was. He was fast losing his patience. "You go home after you clean that," he said. "Harold, you got any news on the prisoners?"

"Oh, cut the goddamn bullshit, O'Connell, and get your ass in here," Sheriff Lester yelled.

Harold's lips firmed. Marcus realized Lester had likely held him accountable for his absence and had come down on him in ways he was damn sure going to find out about. Lester was now standing behind his desk, and Marcus turned away from him, back to Harold.

"I want to know all the details of the last sighting of the prisoner," he said. "Who is still out there, looking? I want to know who's on the ground, everyone who has set foot in my county." He gave Harold a significant look. "Bring it into my office."

He didn't wait for Harold to reply, knowing everyone had heard his order. He started walking to his office, and his wife handed him a coffee.

"Thanks, Charlotte," he said. "You should go home, too. I don't know how long I'll be." He took a swallow of the coffee and felt the tension spike, as it seemed everyone was waiting for something unexpected. Too many law enforcement departments were asserting rights they didn't have in his county.

"You always walk into another sheriff's county and make yourself at home?" he said to Lester as he entered his office. "Get the fuck out of my chair."

Maybe he was too tired to care about being polite. He waited, and the seconds ticked by, Lester staring back at him. He had no idea who he was fucking with, because tired Marcus never backed down from anyone, even someone who was trying to undermine him. Maybe Lester realized, as he pushed back Marcus's chair, stood, and gestured to it.

"You were out of commission for quite a while, Sheriff," he said. "We tracked you. We know when someone's gone dark. So what were you doing? What were you and your brother really doing out there?"

One of the agents, with short, light hair, a medium build, and a smile that wasn't genuine, had walked into his office and sat on his old sofa, leaving the door wide open. What the hell was his name? Butler, Marcus thought. The phones were still ringing, and he spotted

Ryan sitting at a chair by Colby's desk, talking with the other agent, Garner.

"Sounds like you're calling me a liar," Marcus said. "I'd be very careful, if I were you, because what I'm seeing is a bunch of agencies who've overstepped and have no authority in my county. Either of you need a refresher on what a constitutional sheriff is?"

Harold then walked in, with good timing. Marcus took a swallow of coffee and headed around his desk. He set his mug down and took the sheet of paper Harold held out to him.

"This is all I got," Harold said. "The dogs lost the scent at the creek crossing and haven't been able to pick it up. Choppers are still out looking, but no sign. It's as if he just vanished."

Marcus stared at a half page of notes about nothing. He handed it back to Harold. "So we're clear that this is my county, my investigation. Sheriff Lester, you've already overstepped at one crime scene in my county. Holter Donnelly was a street preacher who was shot in the back, so I have to wonder, was the crime scene tampered with? Then there's the question of the bruising all over his body, his face, nothing fresh. Where is the body? I'm going to want a copy of the autopsy. And you do not get to decide, either of you, which laws are and are not enforced in this county."

The agent said nothing, and Lester only pulled his arms across his chest as if he still thought he could push Marcus around. Marcus wondered now how many other sheriffs he did this to.

"Marcus, Marcus, Marcus," Lester said, "let me give

you some friendly advice. We all work together. You haven't learned yet that our team—"

"Don't you ever fucking talk to me as if I'm some wet-behind-the-ears teenager or give me a lecture on teamwork," Marcus said. "You both need to read the Constitution and learn it. My role here is as head of law enforcement for this county, and neither you, nor the state troopers, nor the FBI, nor the Marshals Service have any authority over me or this office. Sheriff Lester, you're out of your lane. I could arrest both of you, and you damn well know it. You will not tell me how to run my office or walk in here and neuter my deputies. They do not answer to you or report to you. You do not get to intimidate the residents of my county or tell anyone here how to do our jobs. And you sure as shit do not get to interrogate me or question my authority. You both know this. I want the body of Holter Donnelly returned, sent over to my coroner to take a look."

"Well, you'll have to work that out with the prison," Lester said. "The body, I understand, was sent back to them. And that's another jurisdiction, since you want to get into who has what rights and where. Holter Donnelly had no rights. He was an inmate with Montana State Corrections, and that supersedes your authority." Lester seemed to really settle into his stance.

For a moment, Marcus thought Butler was finding some amusement in this pissing contest. It seemed as if the wolves traveling in packs hadn't figured out yet that they had misplayed their hand.

"The one with the most authority in law enforcement is the elected sheriff of the county," Marcus said.

"Even the feds and the marshals don't trump that. In fact, in Montana, it's a crime for a federal agent to take any steps in law enforcement without the permission of the county sheriff. Lester, you're out of your county. In case you both missed your geography lesson, this is Park County, so please explain to me where you have my permission. No judge is going over my head. You both know that only the governor has any power to override anything I do or say, and even that I can have overturned.

"I have the power to arrest an elected politician, to arrest anyone I find out has tampered with evidence in my county, has hindered an investigation, or has committed a crime by covering another up. Yet I get the feeling you're trying to bully me and my deputies and impose your will, get me to fall in line so you can control whatever fucking narrative this is."

He made himself stop talking for a moment. He was tired, furious, done with this shitshow. "Either of you come into my county again without my permission, I will take both of you down regardless of your jurisdictional bullshit. Now get the fuck out of my office, and take Garner with you. If either of you is still in my county in the next hour, I will arrest you. You have my permission to search up to my county line for the prisoner.

"You want a statement from me? Here it is: You put a roadblock in my county and arrested Tracy Mitchell, who was helping us find Rafe Jackson. You recorded my conversation over the radio with my deputy when I lost Jackson. Mitchell was in my custody to be questioned. I want her returned now. Any charges against her will come only from this office. You have nothing to hold her and charge her with. Any leads I had were exhausted. Rafe Jackson's father owned a piece of property, which I know you already know about. Ryan and I were there, and no one else was. You had my car towed. It better have been to repair the blown tire. Now call your people. I want Tracy returned now, within the hour."

Butler pulled in a breath and stood up. "She hasn't talked to anyone," he said. "I understand she asked for a lawyer. I'll put a call in to the state's attorney, but I believe charges are pending for aiding and abetting, interfering with an investigation, harboring a criminal, obstruction..."

Marcus unfastened his vest, pulled it over his head, and dumped it on his desk. "I guess you're not hearing me. Tracy Mitchell wasn't obstructing; she was assisting with the investigation in my county. You're charging her with nothing."

"No, Sheriff," Butler said. "We have you recorded, saying you wanted your deputy to pick her up and charge her, saying she'd hidden Rafe Jackson, a prisoner in the state of Montana."

"The truck was his," Marcus said. "I've already interviewed Tracy, and there will be no charges. Anything you have is overreach. Again, my county, my charges, my jurisdiction. Get back in your lane."

The agent actually laughed, and Sheriff Lester's round cheeks reddened just a bit, likely from his anger. Marcus wanted to thank his mom for making all of her kids learn the Constitution. He'd never before considered how important it was.

"That is absolute bullshit," the agent said to him.

Marcus just lifted his mug to him. Just then, Charlotte appeared in the doorway. Harold, watching from the bullpen, had said nothing, but Marcus thought he was trying to hide his amusement.

"Excuse me, Marcus," Charlotte said. "There's a call for you, line three."

"Thanks, Charlotte." He reached for the phone but didn't press the flashing button of the line on hold for him. He let his gaze settle on the fed and the sheriff still standing in his office. His heart thudded.

Sheriff Lester walked out first, and the agent followed him but stopped in the doorway and looked back to him.

"Close the door behind you," Marcus said.

The agent waited a second, then kept walking, and Harold walked over to the door and closed it behind him.

Marcus pressed the line and picked it up. "Sheriff O'Connell," he said, staring at the closed door.

"Sheriff, this is Jim Carlyle, from Stillwater County. I wonder if you have a moment to meet."

Marcus knew the phone was likely still tapped. What had his dad said, wondering how high up this went? Marcus may have had jurisdiction, but there was still plenty of power above him that could crush him.

"Sure, where?" He lifted his watch, seeing that it stopped working. He was tired, he was hungry, and he needed these assholes out of his county.

"Just out front, by City Hall, in the small park."

"Am I going to want to hear this?" Marcus said. His heart thudded again.

"I guarantee it," the deputy said, then hung up, and so did Marcus.

He pulled off his duty belt and dumped it on his desk before pulling open his office door to see Ryan leaning against Colby's desk and Harold walking Sheriff Lester out. Charlotte appeared almost shellshocked.

"Charlotte, I need a clean shirt," Marcus called out. He pulled off his t-shirt, which had dried on him and was damp from sweat, and dumped it on his desk too. He knew it smelled.

"Here, Marcus," she said after fetching a brown uniform shirt, which he pulled on and buttoned up the front. "What happened? They just left. Marcus, what's going on?"

He knew she was worried. He tucked in the shirt and reached for his duty belt again to pull out his SIG, which also needed to be cleaned. "They have a prisoner to look for, and this is my office, my county, not theirs. Told Lester to get back to his county, and the feds too. But now I've got to go. You go home. I'll be there as soon as I can."

He walked back out to Therese's desk and put his gun down. "Therese, I need your gun," he said. "Clean this one for me too, please." He laid his holstered SIG on her desk, and she pulled open her drawer and pulled out her Glock in its leather holster, a smaller one than he was used to. He pulled it from the holster and checked the safety, the rounds, the clip, then shoved it back in the holster and fastened it to the waistband of his jeans. "I have to run out."

"You going to fill me in on what's going on?" she said.

He took in his deputy and remembered what his dad had said. "The prisoner is long gone, who knows where. You clean my gun and lock it in back, then head on home and get some rest. Nothing more you can do."

Marcus walked over to Ryan, who gave him an odd look, and said, "I have to go meet someone. Charlotte can drive you home."

"Be careful," Ryan said. "You sure you don't need me to watch your back?"

Marcus glanced over to his wife, who was closing up her desk, then to Harold, who was in the outer hall, still talking to Lester, who, it appeared, now understood he'd overplayed his hand.

"No," Marcus said. "I think this time, I'll be okay."

CHAPTER 15

Marcus pulled on the ball cap and sunglasses his wife had handed him, likely to hide how rough he looked. He took in the people on the street and in the small park, with green grass, a few trees, and park benches on which usually sat a resident or two. Someone was walking a dog on a leash.

He spotted the deputy off to the side, by one of the newly planted maples, another man with him.

"Sheriff, thanks for coming," Carlyle said.

Marcus didn't say anything. He figured the deputy was close to his age, and the man with him, in blue jeans and a dark blue shirt, a ball cap over his dark hair, was familiar. His face was a darker shade of brown, and his eyes were also dark and watchful. Where had he seen him before?

"Well, I'm here," Marcus said. "What is this about?"

"This is Steven Hardwell, one of the guards from the prison," Carlyle said.

Marcus pulled off his sunglasses and tucked then

onto his hat. "You were at the crime scene last night, standing over the body of Holter Donnelly," he said. He was the guard Rafe had told him about, the one who had helped them escape only to hunt them down.

"I was there," Hardwell said. "I called Jim down after that bullshit story was cooked up. You see, Holter gave himself up. He was injured, barely walking, and he was cuffed and down. I stood him up and had taken just two steps when a shot was fired. He was shot in the back—murder, an execution, whatever you want to call it. It was Peters, a guard who's been a source of misery for a lot of prisoners. Then that fucker, Lester, stepped in and said he'd handle it. He said there was already a shoot to kill order, so there was nothing to see.

"Lester ordered us to move the body. We dragged it about a quarter mile, I suppose, and then he told that deputy, Lonnie, to clean up the scene. I called Jim because I know him and know he'd never be part of this. By the time you showed up, before Jim arrived, Lester had told us that the story would be that Holter attacked Peters, even though anyone who knew Holter Donnelly would know he was the most peaceful, nonviolent man. Even the dog handler wasn't going to argue with the sheriff."

Marcus wondered whether Jim Carlyle had any idea that Hardwell had been the one to get Rafe and Holter out of jail, to help them escape.

Carlyle was quiet, not pulling his gaze from the prison guard until he turned to Marcus and said, "Sheriff O'Connell, they'll try to discredit you. It's already underway. They did that last night, sending out that alert directly to your residents about two dangerous prisoners. Lester figured you were going to be a problem. How do you get rid of a problem that has been elected, someone you can't control?"

He already knew the answer. "You get him unelected any way you can."

"There's more, Sheriff. I hope you know this, and I expect you do, but there's more about Rafe and Holter. Rafe was a vet, watching the back of a street preacher who was stepping on the wrong toes, exposing lies, corruption, and pockets being lined. I've had my eye on Sheriff Lester for a while. I know how he runs his county. The residents, the ones who vote, believe he's looking out for them, but I think they've been too conditioned by a system that isn't working for us. They can't see how corrupt those in Lester's position and others have become.

"Think about it, Sheriff. Who do you take orders from? Where do they come from? Like last night, you got a call from the warden, who'd already gone to a judge, who issued a shoot to kill order, but based on what evidence? How often do you see a judge for a warrant only for the judge to say, 'Yeah, just tell me what you need. We'll waive all the requirements based on your word that you have evidence. Let's just pretend everything is in order, and if it's not, you'll go back and make sure you get it the way it needs to be'?

"The first time Sheriff Lester got a warrant to go in some guy's place and have a look-see, as he put it, I said to him, 'How did you get the warrant? There's no way you had any probable cause.' He just smiled and laughed and said I had a lot to learn. So I've kept notes for years. Steven called me up and asked me to do him a favor and dig up the arrest reports, the files, everything on Holter Donnelly and Rafe Jackson, because he didn't know what was going on. His records, the prison ones, had been altered, as I found out. Do you know who has the ability to alter our records, to change orders, to make evidence disappear?"

Dampness was beading down Marcus's back again. "I'm fucking tired," he said. "Maybe after a good night's sleep and some real food, I'll be interested in twenty questions and tiptoeing around, but right now, I'm not. Rafe and Holter had help getting out. We all know that. Steven, was it you?"

There was silence. Jim didn't pull his gaze from the guard, and Marcus realized they didn't quite know where he stood.

"No bullshit," Marcus said. "This is just us."

Steven leveled him with a frank look. "I've been working in corrections for a decade," he said, "and I've seen a lot of men come and go. The entire system is about breaking them down. The strip searches they do are to humiliate them, that's all. It's all psychological. They have scanners much like you see at the airport, which can see anything on the prisoner anyway. And that's only the beginning of what they do to break them down.

"Corrections staff fall into several camps. Some take great pleasure in having that power over other human beings, hurting them. Others just show up to do their jobs and leave and pretend not to see what's really going on. But a few of us do see the evil of it. People don't understand that when you're a convicted criminal, whether you did the crime or not, those slavery laws that people believe went away suddenly apply to you. You're no longer a person.

"There's no accountability for judges, no consequences for cops once they get away with something. The guards know all the dangerous ones in prison, and some will employ them, use them to teach a lesson, to kill, maim, or do anything they're told to do. The more they get away with it, the bolder they get until they're unstoppable. I'm only one guy. One night, I was told to put a prisoner in a cage and allow him only to sit. He'd been stripped naked, and they'd cranked the heat up so it was a hotbox, no water, no bathroom. It's where they stick only the most dangerous criminals to contain them.

"I was told to ignore his pleas. I saw notes about what a danger he was. But the man I talked to wasn't any of those things. Seven days and seven nights he was locked in there, and guards I won't name laughed at the torture they were putting him through. You know what I learned when I was on alone? That man was more concerned for his friend, a former soldier, Rafe Jackson, than he was for himself. He wanted me to check on him.

"Holter Donnelly was a preacher on the streets, doing what he could to help the unfortunate who lived there because the system worked against them. He said he was dangerous because they couldn't get him to stop digging, helping people, calling out and exposing lies, being loud and vocal, going to the media even though they would never look into what he said. Some business owners may have been sympathetic, but they didn't want to get involved.

"Holter was forced to get a permit to preach. He received dozens of fines, from littering to jaywalking. He got the permit after jumping through hoops and attending all-night meetings of council to pass legislation that changed the rules overnight. He'd been followed by the cops, pulled over for any reason. I saw how far they were going to go. Where the orders came down from, I don't know.

"Prisoners weren't allowed in his cell block, but during the last beating he took, a dozen inmates stepped in. I don't think the guards expected the sheer number of inmates who would stand up for Holter. That was their one mistake. Holter had helped so many of the inmates in there, and even they knew that beating was about breaking him. I suspected there was more. The guards wanted him to sign some confession, saying he lied about what he'd found out about the shelters, the non-profits, the questions he kept asking about the programs, the money."

Jim was looking straight at Marcus, saying nothing, just listening to what the guard said. Marcus was aware Steven still hadn't confessed to helping the two escape.

"You know what goes on in a prison, don't you?" Steven continued. "Like, what really goes on? Solitary confinement is used as torture. There's no innocent until proven guilty. Solitary is concrete, hard benches, no bathroom, no water. They have you naked. They keep it so cold you're shivering or so hot you can barely breathe. They have two cages under the guise of necessity for the most dangerous, the psychotic, the ones they need to contain to get them under control. One cage is just big enough that you can sit. The other is metal, with glass, and smaller. The way it's built, there's not enough air. You can't move.

"Six prisoners came forward to me and said they were offered incentives to hurt Holter, mostly Holter, but sometimes Rafe. It was nonstop, the isolation, the abuse. The nurse would appear with the guard to check on anyone in those cages, always offering drugs, whatever they wanted, cocaine, fentanyl. Most of the prisoners took them. I swear, anyone who goes into jail leaves addicted to something. You know they get paid by the head, prisons and even shelters, like people are cattle?"

The guard made a face, and Marcus could see he was really struggling. He shook his head and continued. "Holter was a good man and didn't deserve what happened. His friend Rafe, too. Damn, he was tough. He only wanted to watch his friend's back. Any beating he got, or punishment, or isolation, was from him trying to defend his friend. I hope to hell they don't find him, because if he's found, he'll never make it back to prison alive. Even if he does, he'll disappear soon after. Whoever is talking to Warden Kellogg, Sheriff Lester, and Judge Harris controls all of them. How high up it goes, I have no idea."

Marcus didn't know why, but he found himself looking up at the bright blue of the early summer sky. "What do you want me to do?" he said. "Sheriff Lester is an elected sheriff under the Constitution. The only one who can remove him is the governor. Your evidence needs to be rock solid. You witnessed with your own eyes the guard pulling the trigger? Romi was there, the dog handler. I don't know him well, but I'm not sure he'd come out against any of them. You're talking about a lot of power. They needed to silence Holter because he was causing problems. So again, I ask you, what do you want me to do?"

Jim stepped forward and held out his hand, and Marcus hesitated a second before shaking it. Jim leaned closer. "Just wanted to make sure you weren't with them," he said. "I needed to know what side you're on." Then he stepped back and rested his hands on his duty belt.

"I'm on my side, the side of the people of this county," Marcus said. "No one owns me. No one." He knew he'd made his point. "If you're going to go after him, you need more than what you think you have."

Something pulled at the corners of Jim's lips. "I know that," he said. "Thanks, Sheriff. Glad to know I've got an ally. The thing is, Sheriff Lester doesn't think I know where the bodies are buried, and neither he nor the warden has any idea that Steven and I have been friends since we were kids. You going to keep searching for Rafe?"

Marcus pulled a hand over his face and heard the scrape of whiskers. "I have a county to protect, Deputy Carlyle. I'll always be looking, but if the trail goes cold and he's no longer in my county, not much more I can do but keep my eyes open." Marcus let his gaze linger on the guard. "So why do you think someone helped them escape?"

Steven maintained his gaze, unsmiling. "When you're in the walls of a prison, you hear things. What was coming down on those two would have them days away from being taken out in a body bag. I'd say someone was watching over them. Again, don't know who did it, but whoever it was, I can't help thinking he did a good thing."

Marcus realized that was all he was going to get. He held his hand out to Steven. "Yes, I'd have to agree you did a good thing."

The guard hesitated only a second, then shook Marcus's hand.

"If it's all the same to you," Marcus said, "I'm tired, and I want to see my family. I'll say goodnight to both of you, and if either of you needs some help, you let me know." He reached for his sunglasses, still tucked on his ballcap, and shoved them back on.

"Sheriff O'Connell," Carlyle said, "they're going to try to take you down any way they can. They will gaslight you, try to discredit you, and run a media shitshow on you."

He didn't know who "they" were, but he already suspected Sheriff Lester would play a front and center role. "Let them try," he said. "The thing is, I plan to be one step ahead of it."

CHAPTER 16

Damn, he was tired. Marcus leaned against the post on his front porch. The sun had set, and all was dark and quiet across the street at Ryan and Jenny's. His brother, he'd been told, had gone to bed as soon as he got home.

In the house behind him, Marcus could hear his son doing his nightly bedtime protest. He spotted headlights coming down the road, and Harold's Kia pulled in and parked in the driveway behind Marcus's old pickup. His sister Suzanne stepped out of the car. Shortly after, Luke pulled in, driving his single-cab pickup. Marcus felt a knot in his stomach, just barely hearing his mom, Reine, and Jenny talking inside.

Suzanne just stood there, letting her gaze settle on Luke as he climbed out of his pickup, wearing blue jeans and an old t-shirt. "Hey, when did you get back?" she said. "Damn, you cut your hair again."

Luke let out a low laugh and walked over and hugged

her, just something he did sometimes. "Just now, barely," he said. "Heard you managed to get yourself in trouble. Harold speaking to you?"

Marcus was positive his sister made a face as they both started walking his way.

"Of course he is," she said. "Who told you?"

There it was, his brother's rough, low teasing laugh. "Oh, a little birdie."

Marcus just took in his siblings. The door squeaked behind him, and he glanced over to see his dad stepping out, wearing a blue and white t-shirt and blue jeans. He let his gaze linger on each of them.

"You made it?" was all he said to Luke, who just shrugged. Marcus had a ton of questions for his brother, but not right now. He glanced over to Suzanne and saw the awkwardness there.

"Suzanne, Harold sleeping?" Marcus said. He lifted his beer and took a swallow.

"Yes, and so is Arnie," she said. "Harold is pretty mad, saying there are fifty ways to Sunday that things could've gone wrong and how just my being there could have screwed things up for you, for him, for the entire sheriff's office, and—"

"You want a job?" Marcus cut in before she could finish. Even though it was dark, the streetlights and the light spilling out from the house was enough for him to see how she stilled, her eyes wide. She was quiet for a second.

"Yes," she said emphatically. Then she frowned, suspicious. "Doing what?"

"Working for me at the sheriff's office," Marcus said.

She started jumping up and down like a little kid, clapping her hands. She threw her arms around Luke, her full weight, before Marcus could even finish. "Yeah! I get to be a cop," she said.

"I didn't say that," Marcus said. "You're not a cop...yet."

He wasn't sure if it was amusement he saw in his dad's expression. Raymond had written the book on how to hold your cards close to your chest.

"So what would I be doing, exactly?" Suzanne said.

"Helping Charlotte, for one. Running interference, handling media relations. First thing, you'll need to get a press conference set up in the morning. Get the reporters there, the local TV stations. I need to fill the people here in my county in on what happened before a bigger media spin can take over, one I think is already well underway."

Suzanne started up the steps with a confidence he hadn't seen in a while and a smile to match. "Okay, I can do that. Marcus, I also suggest sending an alert out tonight by text and a late press release that Sheriff Marcus O'Connell has been on the ground, searching through the night for the escaped prisoners, one of whom was found dead..."

"Under suspicious circumstances," he cut in. "Make sure you add that."

"And that the search continues for one more," she finished. "Then you'll have a press conference in the morning with further details. Don't worry, Marcus. I'm on it. I'll handle it."

He gave his head a shake as his sister pulled open the screen door. His brother Owen was there too, and Suzanne was excitedly telling everyone that she was now working for the sheriff's department.

"You know what you're getting yourself into?" Luke said from where he stood at the bottom of the steps.

"Yeah," Marcus said. "I'm getting someone else who has my back. One thing I know about Suzanne is she's steady under pressure. She's had to deal with some real assholes. I also know she'll be asking for a gun and badge before the week is out." Marcus downed the last of his beer and set the empty bottle on the railing beside him, then pulled his arms over his chest, taking in his brother and his dad, who said nothing. "Do I want to know where he is?" he finally said.

He heard the phone ring inside and thought his sister answered, and he turned to the door and listened for footsteps that didn't come.

Luke pulled an envelope from his pocket and held it out to him. "Always have an exit strategy," he said. "I know mine and can teach anyone to create theirs. Make sure you burn it."

Marcus hesitated only a second before taking the envelope. The screen door squeaked behind them.

"Marcus, that was Colby," Suzanne said. "He said the state troopers left a message about Tracy Mitchell. She was released hours ago, but no one knows who picked her up. I'm on everything else right now. Don't you worry."

Then the screen door closed, and Marcus was very

aware that his dad had pulled a hand over his face to try to hide a smile.

"She always was a go-getter," Raymond said. "Nothing could stop her. She came out that way. She'd just as soon run over a roadblock than go around."

Marcus could hear his sister again inside, on the phone, he thought. She'd likely ask for a key next, maybe rearrange his schedule. Harold would ask him if he'd lost his mind. Marcus squeezed the envelope, blank on the outside and sealed. He wanted to ask what was inside.

"So Tracy was picked up," he said. "Should I wonder by whom?"

Luke looked away and shrugged. "Wouldn't waste too much time on it."

Marcus shook his head. "You know, when I was first hired on as a deputy, I thought I knew so much, but I've only recently figured out that I know less than nothing. Did you know Holter was a warrior who took the beatings and whatever they came at him with? He had to get a permit to feed the homeless. What kind of fucked-up shit is that, in our country? Who does that?"

His dad was looking out onto the street at the houses, the cars, just watching the darkness, something Marcus did too, more and more as of late. Raymond O'Connell had a presence about him when he was quiet, but he could be so big and knew so much about things Marcus had no idea about. He wondered if his dad would ever share those things with him.

Luke pulled his arms across his chest. "Marcus, if you haven't figured it out by now, our government is a mafia that launders our tax money and funnels it right back to themselves. There is no black and white or right and wrong. Sometimes, a man has to die for a while until it's safe for the truth to come out." Damn, Luke could be so cryptic. He started up the steps and slapped Marcus's arm. "Beer inside? Heard you were lagging with Ryan. Getting a little out of shape, being sheriff, sitting behind a desk." Then he pulled open the door and disappeared.

Raymond was still there. Again, amusement pulled at his lips. "You should read your letter and then get some sleep. I'll tell everyone to keep it down." He pulled a lighter out of his pocket and held it out to Marcus, who hesitated only a second before taking it. "You know, Marcus, you're only a threat if they believe you're alive," he said. Then he walked into the house.

Marcus frowned, wondering what the hell he was talking about. He slid his thumb under the seal and opened the envelope to read its contents:

Don't let the truth get buried about Holter Donnelly. If your brother had been my teacher, I'd never have washed out. Tracy says thank you. One day, we'll have a beer. In the words of a wise man who was my best friend and a true hero, "Outlast, outlive, don't ever give in, and never, ever surrender." Thank you. — R

Marcus held the paper and flicked the lighter to the edge, letting the flame burn it down. He reached for the pot he used to scoop out the ashes from the fireplace and dumped the paper inside, just letting it burn, then added the blank envelope.

He realized his son had stopped fussing, and as he listened to the laughter inside, he shut his eyes for a second. He put the lid on the pot after the flames had burned down and tucked the lighter in his pocket, then took one last look at the street before pulling open the door, knowing everyone inside was his family, and they would always have his back.

EPILOGUE

It had been four weeks since Marcus had stood before the cameras and reporters to give his statement on the details of the prison break and the timeline of what had taken place, including the phone call that had come from Sheriff Rourke in Madison County, where they'd found the remains of Rafe Jackson. It was a moment that would forever be burned in his mind, especially as Luke had only slid on his shades in response and said, "No one is looking for a dead man."

He didn't know how his brother had done it. He figured one day he'd ask.

There was a knock at his office door, and it opened before he could say anything. In walked Suzanne in a brown deputy shirt, her hair pulled back.

"Marcus, just got a call from Jim Carlyle. He said to turn the TV on," she said, then reached for the remote and flicked on the TV in his office. Harold stepped inside, too, and so did Charlotte. Therese was on the phone in the bullpen. It took Marcus a moment to realize what he was seeing.

"What is this?" he said.

His sister turned up the sound. "It seems Sheriff Lester has resigned and is under investigation under allegations of racketeering. The investigation has reopened the case of Holter Donnelly, and there's a feature tonight on the pastor who was arrested for fighting for the rights of people on the streets."

Marcus took in the byline running along the bottom of the screen, naming numerous criminal charges against people he'd never heard of before. Suzanne appeared so damn pleased, as if she were responsible for this news. Harold, he could see, was still getting used to having Suzanne take over the station.

Marcus reached for the remote and shut the TV off just as Therese appeared in the doorway and said, "This just came for you, Sheriff."

Marcus didn't get up. Charlotte walked around the desk and took the courier envelope from Therese, then handed it to him. Only his name was printed on the front.

"Thank you," Marcus said. "Why don't you give me the Cliff's Notes, Suzanne, since I'm sure you already know everything and then some of what this is?"

Harold only rolled his eyes.

Suzanne beamed and said, "Well, it seems Fergus County received some anonymous tips sometime back about how Sheriff Lester was pocketing money, skimming off funds meant to be directed to the county jail to feed the prisoners. He's been taking money that was

confiscated under asset forfeiture and has several allegations of excessive force, brutality, falsifying reports,
planting or tampering with evidence... It's a pretty long
list, and the evidence is damning. In the meantime, Jim
Carlyle has been appointed acting sheriff.

"Two people from the Lighthouse Society... Yeah, I
know," Suzanne added at his puzzled expression.
"They're one of many companies no one has ever heard
of that receive state and federal funds and private donations for all kinds of programs to help the underprivi-
leged, from homeless shelters, to meals to go, to camps
for kids, to community outreach. They were basically
caught with their hands in the cookie jar. Their names
are Robert Ashford and Joan Taylor, but that's irrelevant,
because my guess is that they were sacrificed.

"There was a mention, too, about street pastor Holter
Donnelly and how he'd been actively fighting them and
had discovered what they were doing. But here's the
kicker: Our very own governor, Jack Curtis, has just
created a task force on prison reform and corruption in
the prison system. Basically, he's going to be shining a
light on the wardens, the privatization of prisons, the
corrections staff, all of it."

Charlotte slid her hand over his shoulder. "Hey, this
is good news."

"Yeah, I know," he said as he leaned back, looking up
to her smiling face, her smiling eyes.

"Are you going to open that?" she said. "Who's it
from?" She pressed a kiss to the top of his head.

Marcus knew he needed to call Jim Carlyle and
congratulate him. He looked over to his sister and

Harold, who had walked out of the office. Suzanne was laughing. She really did liven up the place.

He ripped open the seal of the couriered envelope and pulled out a picture of a hand holding a beer, a sunset over an ocean, and what looked like a sailboat. All it said as he turned it over was *Cheers*.

"I don't understand. Who is it from?" Charlotte said.

Marcus knew there wouldn't be more. He turned the envelope over to see just his name, so he tossed it in the trash. His wife took the photo, turned it over, and handed it back.

"Who would send you a photo of them holding a beer on a boat?" She made a face. Then she leaned down and pressed another kiss to the top of his head before walking to the door, calling out behind her, "Oh, and we're going to Ryan and Jenny's tonight. The kids want pizza." She stopped in the doorway when he didn't answer.

"Sounds like fun," he finally said. He stood, pulled a tack from the corkboard on the wall behind him, and tacked the photo up, then turned to see his wife raise a brow. He just shrugged. "Great photo. Often thought it would be fun to take a holiday on a boat one day in the middle of the ocean. What do you think, just you and me, some time away?"

She rolled her eyes. "Maybe one day," she said.

He joined her in the doorway and slid his arm around her, taking in Suzanne, who also had her arm around Harold's shoulder. Therese was still on the phone. In the early afternoon, the office was quiet.

"You know what?" Marcus said. "I think I'm going to

be the one who leaves early today. Hey, you two," he called out to Harold and Suzanne. "Ryan and Jenny's tonight. I'm going to head out now and pick up some beer. See you over there."

He gave his wife another kiss. The phone started ringing as he pulled open the stationhouse door, and he stopped for a moment and just stood there, taking in his family. Then he stepped out and started down the hall and outside into the bright sun and blue sky of a gorgeous Montana day. He just had a feeling that every wrong that had been done was going to be made right.

And maybe, one day, he and Rafe would have that beer together.

Turn the page for a sneak peek of
THE CHARITY
Available in print, eBook & audio

THE CHARITY

Some secrets aren't meant to be told.

Police Chief Mark Friessen and his wife, social worker Billy Jo McCabe, keep a watchful eye on their small island town in the Pacific Northwest. As the couple comes to grips with the fact that a hub of crime run by the political elite has turned the quiet, sleepy Roche Harbor into a playground for the rich and powerful, a young executive of a major international charity moves to town. When Mark and Billy Jo dig deep into the secrets and lies that seem to follow the man, they uncover a twisted truth, one they may wish they had never found.

"This was absolutely spell binding. Lorhainne has her reader hooked from the first page and keeps them on the edge of their seats. "

— *L. ZELINSKY*

Newlyweds Mark Friessen and Billy Jo McCabe are back home in the town of Roche Harbor, settling into their life as a married couple while coming to grips with the evil that has woven its web in their small community. Police Chief Mark keeps a watchful eye on all the residents, learning who comes and goes on his island, so when a stranger buys a large property on the west side, Mark shows up on his doorstep to find out why he has moved in.

Walter Crandall tells him the island is home to his five-year-old daughter and his ex-wife, who owns a local bar, and all he wants is to keep a low profile and be left alone to make amends for his mistakes. But there's something about the man that Mark doesn't trust, and when he and Billy Jo begin digging into Walter's past and the charity he was part of, they uncover a deception so twisted they're convinced it can't possibly be true.

THE CHARITY
CHAPTER 1

Sleeping in was something Billy Jo didn't do, but for the past four days, Mark had opened his eyes to find his wife sound asleep. As he stood in the kitchen, the stove blinking a digital blue 8:10 a.m., he realized he needed to wake her soon.

The coffeemaker beeped, and Mark poured himself a cup of the steaming brew before turning back to the island, on which a file lay open, revealing notes on another thirty of the island's residents. Hesitating only a second, he wondered when he'd become that cop who went digging into civilians' lives, looking for any secrets they might have.

Oh, yeah. When a bunch of criminal elites took up using his island as their personal playground.

He had to roll his shoulders, feeling that punch in the gut again, silently hating the world of people who, at times, were untouchable.

"You didn't wake me."

He turned to see Billy Jo in a blue robe, yawning as

she walked sock-footed past him and pulled a glass from the cupboard to fill with water.

"Figured you needed sleep," he said. "Was going to give you another ten minutes before waking you. You feeling okay?"

She brushed her shoulder-length brown bed hair away from her face and shook her head before drinking down the water. "Fine. Just tossed and turned because of your snoring. What are you doing?"

She settled her glass in the sink, then reached for his coffee and took a swallow of it. As she looked down at the open file, her brow furrowed. He realized she wasn't giving the coffee back, and he couldn't believe she had tossed out that comment about his snoring, considering she had fallen asleep before him.

He leaned down and pressed a kiss to the top of her head, then filled a second mug, a matching green one, from the many wedding gifts that seemed to still be arriving daily from people on the island he'd met only a time or two.

"Looking into the folks who live here," he said, "why they live here, what they do, especially the ones who look too clean. Who lives here full time, part time, and what hidden secrets do they have? You know, the usual investigative thing I do, looking for red flags and skeletons."

Mark filled the mug with coffee and settled the carafe back on the burner. Billy Jo angled her head, glancing over to him in that way of hers. She was complex, with many moods, and he figured something else was coming.

"You were serious, then?" she said, flattening her

hand over the file, the notes he'd been reading on Shirley and Tom Campbell, and pulling it closer to her. "You're really going to investigate every person who lives here and dissect their lives even though they've done nothing wrong? Isn't there some law against that, let alone the fact that you're overstepping a bit?"

She didn't smile and didn't pull that fiery gaze from him. She was the complete package, a woman who was his best friend, his lover, his wife, and she knew how to push every one of his buttons. Damn, he loved everything about her.

He reached for the file in front of her and pulled it away. "Knowing who's on this island and what they're about is something I should have done long ago. You forget what happened here? I don't want that kind of evil ever sneaking in. So yeah, I plan to dissect the lives of everyone who lives here to make sure the members of this community are decent, honest, not looking to set up some criminal enterprise, thinking they can do anything. And that includes our politicians. Consider it my new pastime. I plan to find out everything about them, what they do, who they see, to really dig into their lives. If they are honest people, then they become the people I'm protecting. But how many more criminals are still here, so deep underground that I haven't found them yet? And *yet* is the key word."

She looked up at him, and a smile touched her lips as she leaned against the island, so close to him. "You know all the right things to say sometimes," she said. "Go dig and dissect the lives of anyone and everyone. Oh, and make sure, will you, that you take a second and third look at everyone collecting a check from the DCFS, and especially who rubber-stamped their approvals?"

"They're first on the list—kids and animals." He leaned down and kissed her forehead.

"You're the best," she said. "Damn, I'm going to be late." She lifted the mug and took a swallow. "Oh, and I forgot to tell you we're going to drop in and see Gail tonight. I'll swing by the station after I'm done and we'll head over. I told her we'll bring dinner..."

She had trailed off as she walked back to the bedroom. Then she turned in the doorway, looking back, when he hadn't said anything. The tightness that came every time he thought of Tolly Shephard returned deep in his chest. He knew he'd made a face.

"You have to figure out a way to get past that, Mark," she said. "Gail is our friend."

"Her husband was part of a child trafficking ring."

She let out a heavy sigh. "I know what Tolly Shephard did and didn't do—and what they did to his son to gain his compliance when he played both sides. He's dead, but Gail isn't, and she still has to get up every morning and come to terms with all the secrets Tolly had. Mark, you've turned this island upside down and woken up a lot of people to what has been happening behind their backs. No one saw it. The town council is in a state of flux. You have interim appointees, as the mayor and councilors are now charged, awaiting trial. The entire CPS department has been turned upside down, and jobs are still being vacated. You're a hero for the children, Mark, but you have to know many of the island folks have turned on Gail. Their anger is misdirected. Her truck was spray painted with *CHILD KILLER*. People she's known forever on the island have phoned and said some horrible things..."

"Someone vandalized her truck?" he cut in. "Why didn't she call me? When did this happen?"

Billy Jo glanced over to the window. Her three-legged cat was curled up on the cat tree, whereas Lucky had padded into the kitchen and was lapping water out of his dog bowl. She started back toward him in the fuzzy robe that was more warm than flattering, and he didn't know what to make of the shadows around her eyes. He knew well the places her head went when she struggled. What she was thinking, he had no idea.

"Gail won't phone you," she said. "Not that she thinks you wouldn't show up and file a report, because she knows you would, but I think she believes that because of what Tolly did, she deserves every hateful thing coming at her. Yet every time someone lashes out at her, it kills a little piece of her soul. I can see it. I know Tolly wasn't strong enough to end things the way you did. But I also know he hid it well. So tonight we'll take a pizza over, talk to her and be civilized, and let her know she's a human being and we care."

Maybe it was the way she'd said it, but he wondered whether she understood how he felt about Gail. He couldn't look at her without seeing Tolly.

Instead of saying something, he took another swallow of coffee.

"She thinks you hate her, Mark," Billy Jo said, striding back over to him. She put her mug down on the island, not looking away from what he knew was likely shock staring back at her.

"Excuse me?" he said. "I don't hate her. Where would she ever get an idea like that?"

Billy Jo took another step toward him, sliding her hand on the island to touch the file again, likely seeing the names listed. "Maybe it's because you make excuses never to go and see her. I show up alone, and every time I do, she asks about you, and I feel like I'm cheating when I say you're great but busy, or else you'd be there too. She doesn't believe one word of it, because she can see in my face that I'm lying. Or maybe it's because the last time she saw you was when you told her about Tolly."

Mark pulled his hand over his face, knowing she was right. He could feel the heavy sigh of frustration before it passed his lips.

"You going to make me go alone?" Billy Jo said, pulling her arms over her chest, not looking away.

"I don't hate her," he said. "I just don't know what to say to her. There's a difference."

Billy Jo glanced away, pulling in a deep breath. Then she lifted her gaze, which had softened just a bit. "Sometimes just being there is all that's needed. Don't say anything. Don't pretend. Just pick up a piece of pizza and eat. Can you do that?"

He'd never known Billy Jo to be so reasonable. "I can do that."

She ran her hand over his arm, rose up on her tiptoes,

and kissed his cheek. "Good. And you may also want to consider asking Gail to help you dig into the people here. Pick her brain," she said as she reached for her mug and topped it with more coffee.

He wondered if she'd lost her mind. "Breaking bread with Gail is one thing, Billy Jo, but I'm not having her anywhere near this." He knew it had come out rather sharply. He had felt the bite in his words.

Billy Jo blew on the steaming coffee and took a swallow. "Well, that's too bad, because I'm sure she could fill in a lot of holes about a lot of people that you wouldn't otherwise know. And it may help her feel as if she's doing something to make up for what Tolly did. It's a helpless feeling, Mark, feeling responsible even though it's not logical. You could dig and miss something Gail knows that you would never have figured out in a million years. She's been here, like, forever." She tapped his arm again. "Think about it, Mark. That's all I ask."

Then she walked away, and he watched her, her heavy socks, her warm housecoat. This time, she didn't look back.

He reached for the file, seeing the names, as the shower popped on.

"Yeah, there's no way I'm asking Tolly Shephard's widow for help when it comes to anyone on this island," he muttered. Lucky brushed his leg, then looked up at him and whined. "Now, don't go looking at me like that. We'll go see her, eat pizza, and then leave."

There it was again, that sinking feeling he got every time he thought of Gail. As he took in the open file and the notes that only scratched the surface, he couldn't help thinking Billy Jo was too often right. But he wouldn't ask Gail even though she could clear up a lot of questions about a lot of people.

No, involving Gail was exactly what he wasn't going to do.

ABOUT THE AUTHOR

"Lorhainne Eckhart is one of my go to authors when I want a guaranteed good book. So many twists and turns, but also so much love and such a strong sense of family."

— (LORA W., REVIEWER)

New York Times & USA Today bestseller Lorhainne Eckhart is best known for writing Raw Relatable Real Romance where "Morals and family are running themes." As one fan calls her, she is the "Queen of the family saga." (aherman) writing "the ups and downs of what goes on within a family but also with some suspense, angst and of course a bit of romance thrown in for good measure." Follow Lorhainne on Bookbub to receive alerts on New Releases and Sales and join her mailing list at LorhainneEckhart.com for her Monday Blog, all book news, giveaways and FREE reads. With over 120 books, audiobooks, and multiple series published and available at all, retailers now translated into six languages. She is a multiple recipient of the Readers' Favorite Award for Suspense and Romance, and lives in the Pacific Northwest on an island, is the mother of three, her oldest has autism and she is an advocate for never giving up on your dreams.

"Lorhainne Eckhart has this uncanny way of just hitting the spot every time with her books."

— (CAROLINE L., REVIEWER)

The O'Connells: *The O'Connells of Livingston, Montana are not your typical family. A riveting collection of stories surrounding the ups and downs of what goes on within a family but also with some suspense, angst and of course a bit of romance thrown in for good measure. "I thought I loved the Friessens, but I absolutely adore the O'Connell's. Each and every book has different genres of stories, but the one thing in common is how she is able to wrap it around the*

family, which is the heart of each story."
(C. Logue)

The Friessens: *An emotional big family romance series, the Friessen family siblings find their relationships tested, lay their hearts on the line, and discover lasting love! "Lorhainne Eckhart is one of my go to authors when I want a guaranteed good book. So many twists and turns, but also so much love and such a strong sense of family." (Lora W., Reviewer)*

The Parker Sisters: *The Parker Sisters are a close-knit family, and like any other family they have their ups and downs. Eckhart has crafted another intense family drama... "The character development is outstanding, and the emotional investment is high..." (Aherman, Reviewer)*

The McCabe Brothers: *Join the five McCabe siblings on their journeys to the dark and dangerous side of love! An intense, exhilarating collection of romantic thrillers you won't want to miss. — "Eckhart has a new series that is definitely worth the read. The queen of the family saga started this series with a* *spin-off of her wildly successful Friessen series." From a Readers' Favorite award—winning author and "queen of the family saga" (Aherman)*

Lorhainne loves to hear from her readers! You can connect with me at:
www.LorhainneEckhart.com
lorhainneeckhart.le@gmail.com

facebook.com/AuthorLorhainneEckhart

twitter.com/LEckhart

instagram.com/lorhainneeckhart

bookbub.com/profile/lorhainne-eckhart

pinterest.com/lorhainneeckhart

Leave the Light On
In the Moment
In the Family
In the Silence
In the Charm
Unexpected Consequences
It Was Always You
The First Time I Saw You
Welcome to My Arms
Welcome to Boston
I'll Always Love You
Ground Rules
A Reason to Breathe
You Are My Everything
Anything For You
The Homecoming
Stay Away From My Daughter
The Bad Boy
A Place of Our Own
The Visitor
All About Devon
Long Past Dawn
How to Heal a Heart
Keep Me In Your Heart

The O'Connells
The Neighbor
The Third Call
The Secret Husband
The Quiet Day
The Commitment

The Missing Father
The Hometown Hero
Justice
The Family Secret
The Fallen O'Connell
The Return of the O'Connells
And The She Was Gone
The Stalker
The O'Connell Family Christmas
The Girl Next Door
Broken Promises
The Gatekeeper
The Hunted

The McCabe Brothers
Don't Stop Me (Vic)
Don't Catch Me (Chase)
Don't Run From Me (Aaron)
Don't Hide From Me (Luc)
Don't Leave Me (Claudia)
Out of Time

A Billy Jo McCabe Mystery
Nothing As it Seems
Hiding in Plain Sight
The Cold Case
The Trap
Above the Law
The Stranger at the Door
The Children
The Last Stand

The Charity
The Sacrifice

The Wilde Brothers
The One (Joe and Margaret)
The Honeymoon, A Wilde Brothers Short
Friendly Fire (Logan and Julia)
Not Quite Married, A Wilde Brothers Short
A Matter of Trust (Ben and Carrie)
The Reckoning, A Wilde Brothers Christmas
Traded (Jake)
Unforgiven (Samuel)
The Holiday Bride

Married in Montana
His Promise
Love's Promise
A Promise of Forever

The Parker Sisters
Thrill of the Chase
The Dating Game
Play Hard to Get
What We Can't Have
Go Your Own Way
A June Wedding

Kate & Walker
One Night
Edge of Night
Last Night

9 781990 590849